{ A Fool's Paradise }

Anita Konkka

{ A Fool's Paradise }

Translation by
A. D. Haun &
Owen Witesman

Dalkey Archive Press
Normal · London

Originally published in Finnish as *Hullun taivaassa* by
Tammi Publishers, Helsinki, Finland, 1988.
Copyright © 1988 by Anita Konkka
English translation copyright © 2006 by A. D. Haun and Owen Witesman

First edition, 2006
All rights reserved

Library of Congress Cataloging-in-Publication Data available.
ISBN: 1-56478-422-3

This work has been published thanks to the
Finnish Literature Information Centre (FILI).

Partially funded by grants from the Illinois Arts Council, a state agency,
and the National Endowment for the Arts, a federal agency.

Dalkey Archive Press is a nonprofit organization whose mission is
to promote international cultural understanding and provide a forum
for dialogue for the literary arts.

www.dalkeyarchive.com

Printed on permanent/durable acid-free paper, bound in the United States of
America, and distributed throughout North America and Europe.

{ A Fool's Paradise }

{ 1 } I'm sitting at the base of a pine tree writing in a blue notebook. The sun is shining out of a cloudless sky. I hear the drone of the highway from the other side of the bay. When I came to the shore, I saw a white dove, which landed in front of my feet on the path and looked up at me. I felt like it was a sign, but I didn't know what it meant. It had blue eyes like my mother's. There was a black stripe on the edge of its left wing and its left foot was crippled, the toes turned backward. When it took a step, it looked as if it were curtsying to me. A gloomy-looking man is sitting a few meters away watching the sea. He's smoking a pipe. I thought he was the man from next door, come to sit under this tree to wonder why he beat his wife again on Friday night and gave her a black eye even though he loves her. He has the same sort of mustache and sideburns as the man next door, but he's someone else. His wife has probably left him. She's found another man and announced that she doesn't want to live with her husband anymore because he prevents her from achieving self-fulfillment. That's what he's thinking about now, dejectedly. During the night he called his wife while he was drunk and said that he still loves her, but she just said don't be ridiculous. Love is like some oatmeal that the man is trying to force her to eat even though she doesn't want it. The woman slammed the receiver in his ear.

The man doesn't like that I'm watching him. He glares from under his eyebrows and moves farther away. I suppose that no reasonable solution exists for the problems between men and women. Twenty years ago I was sitting on this same beach, unhappily in love with a boy who wrote poetry. He seemed so lonely that I fell in love with him. I thought that he was shy and that was why he didn't call me. I started calling him because I imagined that he loved me. In the end he got tired of it and said that he didn't love me. I wasn't his type. I was too forward. He said he wanted to live his life in a transit lounge, and then he left the country and I haven't heard of him since. A couple of years ago I was waiting in the Frankfurt airport for a flight to Finland and looked carefully, but I didn't see him. The airport had everything a person needs to live, even a bowling alley, a disco, and two counselors. One was a Catholic priest and the other a Lutheran.

The wind has picked up. It drives the froth to the shore and ruffles the pages of my notebook. A red flag is waving beyond the edge of the reeds. Two men are drawing in their nets. Perch or whitefish rise from the sea, as well as a brown Airedale terrier, which shakes its fur and runs over to a girl waiting on the path. The girl is standing against dark tree trunks and is so fair that she looks like she is made out of light. The forest is full of yellow blotches. Two lovers go past arm in arm and a propeller plane buzzes in the sky. The pine that I'm sitting under creaks and groans like an old man; every now and then it's quiet as if contemplating what it should complain about next. At the base of the tree there's a bulge that presses against my backside. I move over to sit at the base of another pine. An ant is dragging a stick three times its own size from the sand. The wind is pushing against the stick at an angle and the ant will have a lot of trouble before reaching the anthill. It never gets there. The sun warms my black skirt. It feels like I'm on vacation from the world.

An old man is walking on the beach, his back ramrod-straight like a general's, carrying a meter-long submarine under his arm with drops of water glistening on its side. The man had been trying it out to see how it works and it must have worked well, because he looks happy. He's been fiddling with it for a couple of weeks, and his wife has been complaining about why can't he find a sensible hobby. Before I start for home, I pick up a stone from the shore. It's speckled and oval, like a bird's egg. I already have a stone from Pasternak's grave in my pocket. It's a reddish chip, one edge of which glitters like gold when you turn it in the sunlight. I've listened to many stones, but I've never heard anything. Stones used to be different. They knew how to talk. Pliny tells us that in Greece certain stones ran away when someone tried to take hold of them, some wept like a child if they were kicked, and some gave out with oracular pronouncements in a voice that resembled a soft whistle.

{ 2 } The morning is beautiful. The sky yellowish and the sun rising from over past the highway. During the night my alarm clock shifted over to the time of some unknown planet. It's 53:90 and the news is on the radio. The population of mother rabbits has increased and unemployment has decreased. The clock moves ahead ten minutes at a time. Maybe it's showing the time on Mercury. The light on the wall grows stronger. The colors in the picture start to come alive; the yellow gladioli glow for a moment. The sun is on its way toward the south; the globe turns on its axis, and in space the solar systems rush toward unknown destinations. It's already 74:20. I woke up in the middle of an exciting dream. I was involved with an international spy who was on the run. He resembled my former boss, who was interviewed on television last night. I never met him and I doubt he even knew that I worked for him. He had so many employees that there was no way he could remember them all. We never saw him in the office, but all sorts of stories circulated about him. On the news program, he said that making predictions is an art that rarely succeeds. He was right. They gave a special storm warning for the Gulf of Finland on the radio during the day. They said that there would be dangerously powerful gusts of wind. But the storm changed its mind and went somewhere else. The trees stood motionless in the yard. The sky was clear. Jupiter shone above the trashcans and the Big Dipper was dimly visible behind the insurance company building.

I read in the newspaper that in Japan the banks have their own astrologers, who predict changes in the relationship between the dollar and the yen from the movements of Mercury and Uranus. I've tried to make predictions too, but I can't predict the future. I've looked at the past, and I know that when Pluto darkened my sun, I lost my job, and when Uranus entered a square with my Venus, my engagement got broken off. I've stared at the stars in the sky until my neck got stiff and I've gone to the bookstore to leaf through the books on astrology. My clothes are still neat enough and not completely out of style, so I don't get stared at there. The time may come, of course, when I can only get into the library. The poor sit there. In the bookstore I read in one guidebook that I have the cross of a mass murderer on my star chart. My father had the same cross. Perhaps we were generals in a previous life. He was an army commander and I was in the air force. He ordered me around, which got under my skin, because I thought I was just as good as him. Mother always said I was my father's daughter whenever I did things she didn't approve of.

By all appearances, I must have had a colorful past. Perhaps I was Jack the Ripper, Landru, or the emperor Nero. I often have dreams in which parts of cities or whole cities are burning. Sometimes only some notable building is burning, such as Parliament, the National Museum or the Ateneum. Once the Helsinki railroad station burned and I was frightened that I was the one who'd set it on fire when I read about it in the paper. Perhaps I set the fire in my sleep. Dreams and reality are so similar that I'm not able to tell them apart. It puzzles me a little that people who claim to remember their past were so often kings and queens. Do they have better memories than ordinary people? One completely sane woman remembered having been Anne Boleyn. She went to work in a New York advertising agency and immediately felt a powerful attraction for—and at the same time a horror of—her boss. Only later did it turn out that the boss had been Henry VIII. Another woman was in love with a man whom she didn't dare marry and couldn't understand where the hesitation was coming from until she recalled that she had been Elizabeth I and the man had been the Duke of Leicester. Asylums are full of former emperors and kings. Maybe their sense of time has just gotten mixed up and they don't remember who they are in the present.

The wheels of the mail cart rattle in the yard. After a moment the mail slot clacks. The mail consists of the Paper Workers' Union magazine and an invitation to a research seminar. Someone is lecturing on the subject: "The Problem of the Biographic Form in Virginia Woolf and Thomas Mann's *Doctor Faustus*." I was supposed to become a scholar. My professor encouraged me, but then she burned to death and I stopped going to seminars. I was researching Finnish women's portrayals of men from the period of the Kanteletar folk songs to the modern era. It's been three or four years since then, but the invitations still keep coming. Nowadays I research my pockets to see whether somewhere at the bottom there might be even one mark, but I haven't found anything but fuzz, small stones, and a single magpie feather. You find everything but what you're looking for. Once I was looking for a black button in my sewing box, but I found a gold ring. There was no inscription on it. I took it to a pawnshop, paid the electric and telephone bills, and bought some black buttons.

I'm flipping through the Paper Worker's Union magazine while waiting for the tea water to come to a boil. The magazine is addressed to the previous resident and has been coming for fifteen years. The cat opens the kitchen cooling-cupboard and sits waiting for a bird to fly into her mouth. She remembers that one autumn at about this same time, when the days were growing shorter and the ground was covered with frost in the mornings, a sparrow flew out of the cooler. Now she sits in front of the door hour after hour. Our life passes in sleeping and waiting. At night I wait for sleep to come and the final truth to be revealed. So that I'll become wise during the night and understand what this world is. In the morning I wait for the mail to come and bring a solution to the problems of existence. For my great aunt who went to America at the beginning of the century to have found an oil well or to have married a millionaire, and for me to inherit her fortune. But nothing ever happens when you wait.

{ 3 } The forest smelled of mushrooms and dead leaves. There was a spruce cone in my basket. I trudged along through the trees behind Alexander. His basket was half full of mushrooms. We were in his forest, which was owned by the city. He had been picking mushrooms here since he was a child and knew right where they grew. I call him Alexander, because in a dream I saw a man who was like him. It happened before I met him. The man was fat and had a big nose and he was wearing a plaid overcoat. He was standing waiting for a bus at the Huopalahti Road stop. I married him. It happened suddenly, like falling in love. His name was Alexander Tiilikainen. Another man came toward us on the path and said that the nature books are all mixed up now. He'd seen a bat flying in the middle of the day. Alexander had seen a bumblebee whose wings had withered up. They chatted about the state of nature for a moment, then the man continued on his way. Alexander glanced at my basket and said, "You must not be on good terms with the forest sprits, since they're not giving you any mushrooms."

I lost my temper. My eyes were open and I began to see that under the aspens there were small mounds of leaves that rose up from the ground like molehills in a field. Under these grew the dingy agarics, with caps the same color as the aspen trunks. Alexander got his basket full and we started for home. While we were cleaning the mushrooms, I thought that it was a good idea to get married to a man who can find mushrooms and listens to Channel One on the radio: at least there's no fighting about radio programs when picking mushrooms together isn't fun anymore. I wonder what kind of man Alexander is but I can't figure him out. He's so complicated, and I only see him from one perspective: rose-colored. He's as round as an ostrich egg. He weighs two hundred and twenty-two pounds, his shoes are size nine and he smokes Russian-style cigarettes. There are holes in his shirts. At night he talks in his sleep. There's a little of the prophet in him, but I don't believe his predictions; he doesn't believe them himself until they come true. He gives me food and wine, slices cucumbers, fries the mushrooms and cooks rice. He makes plates out of a milk carton. You get two disposable plates when you cut it lengthwise and fasten the pieces together. When he was young he invented the airplane and applied for a patent for it, but the airplane had already been invented. His worst quality is that he's married. His wife's name is Vera and she doesn't live in Finland. Vera is a strange person. Sometimes she wants a divorce, sometimes she doesn't. She's like the capricious women in Dostoyevsky's novels who torment men, because some man corrupted them when they were young. Alexander doesn't want to divorce her. Generally men don't divorce—they take a mistress, who helps them endure the difficulty and pain of marriage. In the past mistresses were stoned to death in the marketplace and somewhere in the world that still happens. I can understand that a betrayed wife would toss stones, but not people who don't have anything to do with it.

I stayed overnight at Alexander's place. The wind shook the apple tree outside the window. I can't describe what happens when a man and woman come together. It's a mysterious event. A spirit enters the body and makes it move. It's as ordinary as turning on a light. He spoke some beautiful phrase, but I've forgotten it. Afterwards I was sad. I mourned that I had to fall in love, even though I know that love hurts.

In the morning we told each other our dreams around the kitchen table. I had been looking at the starlit sky and saw the seven stars of the Big Dipper, which had started to move and settled down in a row, one after another. Above them the North Star shone large and bright. Alexander told about having danced with a strange woman. According to his mother's dream book it meant sorrow, but the stars predicted success for me. My destiny will be fulfilled with the help of some friend of the opposite sex, it said in the book.

He looked out the window, depressed, and said that the robins had come. I read in the newspaper that 94% of Finns are satisfied with their lives. Only every twentieth is dissatisfied, but every fourth is disappointed with her family life. Those statistics were gathered by the agency where I worked.

"There were five hundred people and only one was happy."

"Was it you?"

"No, it wasn't me; it was the office's message boy."

In his opinion, I was a happy person. Perhaps I am nowadays, but I wasn't when I worked at the agency. Some injury from that period got lodged in my soul, because I have nightmares that I still work there. I'd been there three years when my temporary employment contract didn't get renewed for some reason at the end of the year. They don't always tell you why. In one movie they tried to kill Buster Keaton because he was McCoy's son. No one knew what McCoy had done wrong; it had been something serious, because they still had to take revenge. Perhaps Anneli, who was my immediate supervisor, had found deficiencies in my work. Maybe I didn't seem diligent enough. In office meetings she stressed that everyone had to look busy and that you couldn't stand idly in the hall, because she'd heard from reliable sources that the public relations office has too many high-paid bureaucrats that don't do anything. I didn't stand around idly in the halls, but I probably gave some incorrect information to people who were inquiring about the construction cost indices, wholesale trade volumes, the national defense budget's share of the gross national product, and the OECD countries' investments in petroleum. I tried to the best of my ability to respond to the thirst for information and I didn't give incorrect information deliberately, but statistics are like train schedules. Errors happen easily when there are so many columns and the pages are full of small black numbers that look as much alike as flies.

{ 4 } The sun was just shining; now it's getting dark. Black clouds are coming from the north. I haven't done anything useful today. Lao Tzu said that the world is the workshop of spirits, where one mustn't act, because it is corrupted by action. The unemployment authorities have a different philosophy. They send me letters about temp positions—standing in for office secretaries on maternity leave—but I don't reply.

I met a man on the shore who said he was a surgeon. He got eight thousand marks of social security a month, but he was temporarily so poor that he bummed three cigarettes from me. He came out of the woods carrying a long-handled broom, at the end of which was dangling an Alko liquor store bag, and sat down next to me at the base of the pine tree like an old friend. He had bright eyes and an intelligent expression; I wasn't afraid of him, even though he was like Diotima's Eros: a barefoot, roughly built, dirty and homeless creature that hangs around in alleyways and in front of doors. I talked to him about the newspapers. He was of the opinion that the Helsingin Sanomat was the country's best paper. It was thick, warm, and absorbed moisture well. His name was Vasily; I didn't find out his last name, because his front teeth were missing. He asked me what my name was, and I said Katri Kuusinen; that's what I always say when someone asks. Vasily said he was from far away in Russia. He asked if I believed that he was from where he said he was. I looked at him carefully and figured that he looked as much like a Russian as Finns do generally. He said that he loved women and danced on the beach like Zorba the Greek. Two elderly women were passing along the path. One bent over to whisper in my ear:

"Watch out for that man. He's violent."

Vasily ran after the women, who fled for dear life. I don't know what happened to them because I left. If they hadn't been afraid of Vasily, he wouldn't have chased them. Lunatics and drunks know what people think of them and behave according to their expectations.

Now I'm sitting in the shoreside café and thinking that the exterior is a manifestation of the interior and everything visible is just symbolic.

"Fingernails get more brittle with age," says an old man to his wife.

I can't see them. They're sitting behind me. A man in a blue sweatshirt is reading the evening newspaper and chasing away the sparrows that land on his table. He isn't a bird lover.

"Using the restroom costs a mark," says the old man behind me.

He isn't as old as I'd imagined based his voice, nor is the woman his wife, because he asks her whether she still has those brown plates at home. The man shows the woman how his pocket calculator works and says that it's a good idea for the woman to buy herself a desk model, because it's much sturdier. They don't sound like lovers. Perhaps they're family, or co-workers who will only later fall in love with each other.

"It's already one-thirty," the man says.

They get up and leave. Two women come to the next table and talk to each other in hushed tones. They feed the sparrows. One says that at home she doesn't give the animals food from the table.

"I'm so glad that I can be alone and have peace and quiet," says the other, looking sad.

She doesn't know that she's sad. Only years later, when she thinks of this autumn, will she remember that she was sad about ending up alone. Civilized people don't reveal their feelings even to themselves—they consider these too common. But it confuses me when they say something different from what they think and feel. You can't trust them or be comfortable in their company. I'm talking about myself, because I'm civilized too.

The black pen casts a clear shadow on the paper when I write. The shadow of darkness is light. Three men are standing on Fisher's Croft wharf. Their dark silhouettes are outlined against the sun. They've been at an important business meeting. Now they're climbing into a hydroplane, which rocks on the waves, looking as light as a cork. When I was a child, I couldn't understand why ships stayed on the water's surface and airplanes in the air even though they're made of iron, when I, who am only made of skin and bone, can neither fly nor walk on water. The engine starts and the machine takes off; the sun flashes on its wings. It slides along the surface of the water like a gigantic June bug. At the opposite shore it turns into the head-wind, begins to rise, is already in the air and flies toward the sun. A streetcar circles toward its final stop. A screeching noise comes from its wheels. The streetcars used to rattle more, now they hum like electric trains, but the crackle of the overhead cables is still the same. In Munich and Moscow the streetcars are blue, in Frankfurt they're white and in Stuttgart, yellow. Of all the foreign cities I've visited, Stuttgart felt the most familiar. I lived on the side of a street a streetcar ran along. Its sound was a part of my sleep, and I felt secure, as though I'd come home. The feeling was the same as when I was a child, when I got back to the city after summer vacation ended, got to sleep in my own bed again, heard the streetcar go rattling by under the window. The terrors of rural life were behind me and life was back on the right track.

{ 5 } Alexander once said that I was like a sleepwalker when we met. His words came back to me when a girl walked into the café, sat down next to me, and asked for a cigarette. I didn't notice anything odd about her at first. She lit the cigarette, held it affectedly between her fingers, sprinkled ashes on me, and muttered phrases that I couldn't make out. I thought that she was speaking to me, but I was really only a minor disturbance in her sleep when I asked,

"Excuse me, what?"

"I didn't say nothin'," she answered curtly and continued her muttering.

Maybe she was crazy but didn't know she was. People don't notice those kinds of things themselves. In a dream, sometimes it will flash into your mind that this must be a dream, and usually you wake up at the same moment you realize you're dreaming. The same thing probably happens with insanity. Your head clears up when you notice that you're insane.

In my own opinion, I was wide-awake when I met Alexander. I remember that it was a sweltering evening and I had on a green silk shirt, a sun hat and sunglasses, which made me look silly-sweet like a robin. I climbed onto the bus at the second stop on Huopalahti Road. Alexander was sitting in the door seat and I didn't notice him because he was too close. He recognized me but didn't say hello. Later, when I asked him why he didn't tug at my sleeve, he said that you aren't supposed to wake sleepwalkers—you could scare them to death. I went to sit at the back of the bus. I always sit above the left rear wheel, because someone said once that it's the safest place. I saw him from there and thought that I'd go ask him how he was doing. The last time I'd seen him was on the train when he was coming from Vera's place. Depressed, he said that Vera had demanded money and that he didn't have any. I moved over to sit next to him. His life had taken a turn for the worse. Now Vera was demanding a divorce and hadn't wanted to see him for seven months.

"Where are you going?" he asked.

"To get a drink," I said.

We went together and drank two bottles of retsina. I behaved with decorum—I didn't knock over the glasses and didn't come on to him, because one time I made an ass of myself when I came on to a guy. I was so young then that I didn't know how a woman was supposed to act. We discussed the geopolitical situation and Vincent van Gogh's ear with some photographer who said that he was the reincarnation of van Gogh. When you looked carefully, he did have a little of the same look. It didn't occur to me to begin a relationship with Alexander and so I was quite surprised when he kissed me under a dentist office's sign as we were leaving the restaurant.

The god of that moment seized him and commanded him to kiss me. In the zodiac of the soul, the stars collided and seized each other by their points. The sky was orange-yellow; the sun had sunk beneath the horizon. It was in the House of Love. On the eastern skyline, the moon and Jupiter were rising in the constellation of Aquarius; Uranus ruled in the middle of the sky; and in the west, Venus and Mercury were sinking beyond the horizon. If some child happened to be born at that moment, he would've gotten a beautiful star chart as a birthday present. A kite was flying in his sky, with the sun holding it at the end of a string. He would become a psychoanalyst, an astrologer, or a clairvoyant, and he would grow taller than his parents.

What sort of future might a relationship have that was born on a street corner? Divination is arithmetic, and I did poorly in that subject in school—I had to go to summer school and got held back a year. I didn't learn to understand logarithms, sines, cosines, or square roots. How could I learn to understand fate, then? I see a shadow, but I don't know if it's the shadow of the past or the future. I don't know how to tell them apart. In the subconscious there is no time, and my memory is short, my imagination limitless. The subconscious knows. Sometimes it answers when you ask, but its answers are like an oracle's perorations. I can't comprehend them. I asked it once if I'd met Alexander in a previous life and what had happened between us. In a dream a black lizard with a golden pattern on its back appeared to me. It walked on its hind legs and raised one foreleg up in the air like a traffic cop. In the background a man was talking who had a voice like a nature film commentator: "It is the gecko that won't tell."

In ancient times the Chinese kept geckoes as pets, because they rid the house of vermin, and a magical poison was obtained from them when they were put into a pot on the fifth day of May and fed with sinopia powder for a year. They were killed and the arms of young girls were marked with the substance obtained from them. The mark disappeared when the girl had sex with a man. Husbands marked their wives when they left on long journeys. Men didn't need to be marked because they didn't get pregnant, and, anyway, they were more faithful than the women, at least in their hearts.

When I had the dream, I didn't know that geckoes were used for things like that. I read about it later and began to think that either Alexander or I had been an unfaithful wife, and the marriage had ended unhappily, and the gecko didn't want to tell so that we wouldn't start to hate each other for no reason. When I went with him to Loviisa to look at houses last summer, I was on the verge of remembering something from our past. He was standing on the pier talking with some local. A silent black osprey circled in the sky, and the local's son floated a black umbrella in the water. I watched Alexander as if through the lens of a camera, and he started to look like a Chinese merchant. Pictures formed in my mind like something I'd seen long ago in a film or a dream. I lived in a Chinese port city and saw a lane with many people and a small room, the floor streaked with shadows from the Venetian blinds. It was hot and dark in the room. He stood in the doorway. I couldn't see any more.

{ 6 } On my way back from the employment office, I dropped by the university's botanical garden. When I was a child I went there with my mother to look at the giant water lily, and I burned my nose on the hemp nettle, because I wanted to know what it smelled like. The dried leaves rustled; the wind drove them before it. The scent of piñon wafted in from somewhere, and I felt a longing for sunnier lands and happier people. I walked along the paths and read the names of the plants. Next to a larch was a plaque that said "Hazelnut Tree"; and at the base of a pine it said "European White Elm." Next to the wall of the greenhouse was an ugly, crumpled bush with branches that resembled worms and brown leaves that curled inward as if the bush was suffering from some chronic disease. It didn't have a Finnish name. Perhaps it was suffering because of its outward appearance, like a person with crooked legs, squinty eyes, and a potato nose, I looked at it sympathetically. Perhaps it was happy for a moment, when it noticed that someone was paying attention to it. The greenhouse cost three marks, but I didn't have that much.

I didn't get to see if the giant water lily was still there.

I left the garden and was casually walking along Kaisaniemi Street when I saw a woman standing on the corner of Vuori Street. She looked like my stepmother. I was startled and moved to the other side of the street and didn't dare look to see whether it was really her or someone else. I haven't seen her since my father's death and that was nearly ten years ago. At the estate inventory she said some things that I haven't forgotten or forgiven. She said that I was a pampered, spoiled princess, who regarded her as a parlor maid and kitchen servant, ordering her to carry the deck chairs to the yard and freshen my coffee. The pupils of her eyes contracted to the size of pinheads when she said that I was a snake that had slithered its way into her marriage and destroyed it. I didn't understand what she meant. After all, she came after me and robbed me of my father.

I didn't choose her like I chose my parents, when I felt like being born. I looked through a gap in the clouds to see where to be born and saw a dark-haired young woman on the shore at Kaivopuisto, walking alone and looking sad. She was troubled because she'd fallen in love with a married man, whose wife had gone insane because she'd studied too much astrology. The man couldn't desert his insane wife, since in his opinion it would be unethical, but he couldn't leave the young woman he was infatuated with either. He languished between the two women and at times was so desperate that he contemplated suicide.

I thought Mother was unique in a familiar way—there was a bit of the mystic in her, a bit of the Oriental woman. I fell in love with her at first sight and crept from heaven into her womb. I had rigged the game to Mother's advantage, but I feel like Mother never forgave Father for not choosing her of his own free will, and Father never forgave himself for deserting his first wife. After a few years, they began to make life difficult for each other. They didn't blame me, even though I had caused the whole mess when I pigheadedly decided to be born. They blamed each other.

The sky is darker than usual tonight, and the stars and the moon are nowhere to be seen. I've gotten used to them already. On the opposite hill, on the upper floor of the high-rise, a chandelier is burning. My lamp has a cardboard shade. It reminds me of Mother's pleated skirt. Someone is going up the stairs and beer bottles clink. Before, milk bottles clinked. They were brown and had red foil lids. Mother skimmed the cream from the mouth of the bottle into her coffee with a tiny spoon. She sat at the kitchen table, secretly ate potato pastries and frowned angrily if anyone bothered her while she was drinking her coffee. When I think of Mother, I see a picture like this: on the top of a mountain is a tall tower and at the top of the tower, a narrow window with bars in front of it. Mother sits behind the bars and looks at the sky. She sings that her homeland is on the other side of the stars. She wasn't really at home in this life and that's probably why she died young. I long for her often, but never miss my father, because Father is in me and I'm in him.

A quarrelsome relationship with one's mother causes longing, and lurking behind it are subconscious, sadistic fantasies, or so said a book called *Itching and Scratching*. I borrowed it from the library because I wanted to know what was making me itch during the final months I worked at the agency. Like a swarm of mosquitoes under my skin, stinging constantly. My dreams weren't good either. I'd ended up in a war that continued from one night to the next. From the itching book I found out that I had aggression, feelings of guilt and shame, as well as exhibitionistic tendencies, which I had repressed. The writer was some Freudian psychoanalyst. When you read them, you don't need to get married. They tell me what kind of woman I am deep down; no illusions are left. I'm not a mature woman because my prime need is to love a man, not to be loved. To a mature woman, focusing on objectivity isn't important. She wants to be admired for her being and not because of her actions. She attaches herself to a man genuinely, doesn't envy him and doesn't compete with him. I am powerless and confused, at times unhappy as well. One friend gave me the advice that when I find myself in the power of these feelings, I should raise my left hand into the air, and an angel will take hold of it and help. I raised my left hand. It felt light and cool, as though a slight breeze had crossed my hand, but when I lifted my right, it felt stiff and lifeless, and the air didn't flow around it. I thought I heard an angel whisper in my ear, "Suffering is absurd." It must have been a Buddhist angel. Christian angels teach that three things crown a person. They are: suffering, guilt, and death.

Today, no kind of angel takes my hand, although I'm standing with my hand held up in front of the window and watching the pine tree with its branches being swayed by the wind. A blue bus stops at the base of the pine tree. On the side of the bus it says, "Here goes a can of Finns™." At least one looks Japanese. The people sit straight-backed and look serious. They don't look out of the bus windows. Mother has forbidden it. Now if someone would happen to glance in this direction, he'd think that I was crazy, and he wouldn't be very far off. I enjoy looking in people's windows and thinking about what kind of lives they lead. To some extent I'm a voyeur as well as being an exhibitionist, even though I don't frighten innocent men by stepping out from behind trees naked when they're jogging on the paths in the woods. People have the annoying habit of drawing the curtains in front of their windows when evening comes. What secrets do they have? What vices are they indulging in behind those closed curtains? They probably don't do anything stranger than scratch their heads and pick their noses while watching television. If people knew everything about each other, then everyone would gladly forgive both themselves and others, and there wouldn't be any pride or arrogance among people, said Hafiz, but he was a poet. They always daydream about impossibilities.

{ 7 } The cover of the mailman's cart bangs in the yard. A moment later the mail slot clacks. A reminder card from the library comes, and a letter from an employer. The library is demanding Claude Simon's *The Georgics*, which I don't remember having borrowed. The employer thanks me for my interest in the information specialist's job that was open at their company. He tells about having endeavored to choose from among the applicants the one whose goals, abilities, and qualifications would fit his organization's requirements and laments that the choice has not fallen on me this time, but he will be glad to keep my application papers in case the company needs the contributions of someone like me in future. He's a long-winded employer; usually they just thank you for your interest when they return your application.

I look through the help-wanted ads in the newspaper and think about what I might do. The Deaconess Institute is looking for a public relations officer, and some advertising agency is looking for a creative individual who is ready to dive head first into the product and consumer world—everything from toothpicks to social services. One time I figured that I was a creative person and applied for a position as a copywriter, but I didn't get any reply. After I mailed in my application, I had a nightmare the next night, where I was running for my life from an ad-man who was demanding that I think up a detergent ad. "Omo whitens, Omo brightens," came to mind, but it wasn't good enough. Just as he was about to catch me, I woke up and realized that advertising wasn't for me.

I went to the library and found out that I'm the victim of a computer. The clerk said that so many books are being checked out nowadays that their computer doesn't have enough capacity and that mistakes occur constantly. She looked exhausted. Her hair was disheveled and there were red blotches on her cheeks as she cleared away the mountains of books that had collected on the circulation counter while I'd been interrupting her. I'd read in the newspaper that a contagious virus more dangerous than AIDS is threatening the world's computer population. In the same day's newspaper there was a report about a study on changes in workplace life. The researcher was of the opinion that the use of microelectronics contains mystical elements. "It feels like there's something smoldering under the surface," he said.

The Georgics was on the shelf, and I checked it out, since it had announced in advance its desire to be checked out. Judging by its stiffness, it had never been opened. It belonged among the library's outcasts. People are peculiar about wanting to borrow the same books as everybody else. Sometimes somebody takes an unknown book in hand, leafs through it and puts it back on the shelf. Whenever I see someone reject a book, I hurry over to it. That's how I found Rilke's *The Notebooks of Malte Laurids Brigge*, Yeats's memoirs, and, most recently, Cesare Pavese's diary. On the cover was an ugly, bespectacled man with a large nose, a cigarette butt dangling from his mouth and a beard that looked as though it hadn't been shaved for at least two days. I understand that a face like that can't please everyone. There are people who prefer to read beautiful writers, but I'm not choosy when it comes to external appearances. When I took Pavese's diary from the shelf, it opened to a place where I read: "Young man, stop grieving after you lose your beloved. This has happened to every man, that a woman has rejected him, but they haven't broken nor gone insane." When I read that, I thought that both genders have the same feelings—is there any difference other than the fact that there are nine holes in a man and ten in a woman?

On my way to the library I met two mysterious men. I had thought about one of the men last night, before I fell asleep: was he dead? I hadn't seen him for a few weeks. His name is The Prophecies Shall Be Fulfilled, because he had a book with that title under his arm when I saw him for the first time. He's in his sixties or seventies; he could even be slightly older, because I can't estimate men's ages very precisely. He's tall and thin, his posture is stooped and his clothes are worn out. He has a dog-fur cap on his head. His cheeks are hollow and his eyes glimmer like water in a deep rock crevice. He looks like a lonely man, perhaps his wife died years ago, or he never had a wife at all. He gets onto the bus at the second stop on Huopalahti Road and gets off at the railroad station square, or the other way around, if he's coming from the city. He seems to follow the same schedule that I do even though I haven't had a regular schedule for nearly a year. Maybe an invisible connection exists between us. When I decide to go into town, he does too. He pulls on a coat and galoshes, puts a cap on, takes a book under his arm and dodders across the street to the bus stop. Today the friendly glimmer of a smile appears in his eyes. He has never acknowledged me by any expression or gesture before. Perhaps he thought that I had moved away, or died, and he felt happy when he saw me. The feeling was mutual. Under his arm was the book *Illustrated Birds of Scandinavia*; in my hand were *The Georgics* and D. H. Lawrence's essays about the unconscious and the imagination.

I met the other man in front of the library. He was also old. He gave me a white tulip and wanted to take a photograph, but there was no film in his camera. He had neat, dark clothes, a white shirt and a black tie. I didn't ask if he had been on the way to some friend's funeral, been late, and not dared to take the tulip home because his wife would have started to ask where he'd been loafing around all day, since he obviously hadn't been at the funeral. The tulip had wilted from lack of water. I put it in a green St. Remy bottle and now its stem is reaching perkily toward the ceiling. The ceiling has footprints on it like a dog or fox has been walking there. I've often wondered where they came from, but never figured it out. There are a lot of things in this world that can't be explained.

{ 8 } I was in my twenties when I met Alexander for the first time. He appeared before me unexpectedly from between the shelves of the Elanto grocery store and asked if I worked there. I didn't answer; I glared at him crossly and turned my back. I didn't like him; he was a handsome man and smiled conceitedly. I thought that he was trying to hit on me. In those days when men talked to me, that was all they had on their minds. Some asked for directions, some asked the time, but in the end they still always asked if I'd go with them to gaze at the moon. I went with some, too. Alexander explained later that he thought I was a salesgirl, because I had a green coat on. The mistake embarrassed him afterwards. He didn't know what had gotten into him. It became clear last night when I was reading Lawrence's essays. Lawrence writes that a woman sends a dark, intense invitation through the air. Some man who has the same vibration frequency senses the call in his spinal cord. The man's daytime consciousness and sight become dim, and he drifts helplessly into the woman's magnetic field. There's a natural explanation for everything, and if there isn't, someone invents one. But what I don't understand is why I didn't run into Alexander at all for fifteen years, even though we walked on the same streets, knew the same people, traveled in the same buses. I met him for the second time in the No. 6 streetcar. I didn't recognize him because he didn't look the same as when he was young. He introduced himself and asked me how some of our common acquaintances were doing. I didn't know because I hadn't seen them since my student years. We didn't talk about anything important, but I was so thrown off by meeting him that I inadvertently got off the streetcar a couple of stops too soon. I wondered why he came to talk with me. I thought that it was because of my colorful wool jacket, even though that didn't seem like a very logical explanation. That night I had a nightmare. I woke up to a commotion echoing from the stairwell. When I went to see what was happening there, I saw that the outside door's lock was broken open, the door was ajar, and there was a black handbag sitting on the grating that served as a doormat. I felt like something terrible must have happened. In the morning there was a stabbing pain in my right temple, which developed into a headache that lasted three days. I wrote that sorrows come in a black bag, and that falling in love happens during moments when you don't realize you need to be on your guard. When you notice that it's happened, there's nothing you can do. I was so close to falling in love then, but when I wrote that, I wasn't thinking of Alexander, nor did I know that he had married Vera half a year earlier. I presumably didn't even know that his first wife had died.

Mysterious currents of thoughts and feelings flow between people, and they know more about each other than they believe they do. I can't see any farther than my own nose, but something lives inside me that sees and arranges events in my life: something that knew what would happen two years ago when it forced me into motion in the middle of cleaning. The water bucket and mop remained on the kitchen floor. I put on my city clothes and started for the bus stop at a run. The driver stepped on the gas. He was having a bad day or just wanted to torment people. It was probably because of the heat wave, I thought at the time. Now I think that there is no such thing as coincidence. Everything has some diabolical purpose. Once I ended up in Stuttgart, even though I was on my way to Munich. I got on the wrong train. It was a beneficial mistake, because I met an old friend in Stuttgart. He taught me how to consult a Chinese oracle for advice. When he was young he taught me how to listen to Bach and Mozart. If you were to always only meet people you'd been planning on meeting, nothing new would happen. But why do I think so much about beginnings nowadays? Is it a sign of the end? Lot's wife turned into a pillar of salt when she looked back, and Orpheus lost Eurydice. When you fall in love, you become superstitious and start to see evil omens in everything. You're like a sailor at the mercy of the forces of nature.

{ 9 } Two intersections and part of an old gravel road are visible from the window. Now it's a park path. I often have dreams about that road. Its name was West Street. It began in the south on the seashore, and in the north it joined the road leading to Turku. There was a gravel pit beside it, with swallows' nests in its side. I got sand for the cat there when I was a child. Now there's an insurance company building there, but I can't see it from the window because the bunker-like health center is in front of it. The arm of a crane swings around behind it. The cat moves back and forth along the arm. I don't know what the technical name for that part is, where the cable that lengthens and shortens is attached, but it's called the "cat." If I lived on the top floor, then when the trees are leafless I would be able to see Alexander's building, which has four corner apartments. Perhaps I'll move there to live, because a Gypsy on the boat to Sweden predicted that I would grow old in a corner apartment or a corner building.

Life is straightforward. I'm slowly moving toward the north. I measured on the phone book map that during my life I've progressed two or three kilometers. Even a turtle is faster than me. I haven't deviated to the right or left, to the east or west, because the three buildings I've lived in lie on the same line. I was born near the sea. I lived for twenty years on the corner of Park and West and now I'll grow old on the corner of Ulvila Road.

Today I'm a year older than yesterday. During the night I turned thirty-eight. At this age, it's possible to be born again. The next chance isn't until age fifty-six. Being reborn means that a person sees her fate in a new light. For a long time I thought that I didn't have a fate. I was so inconspicuous, not even waiters saw me. Usually I ended up leaving the restaurant with an empty stomach, and dead sober.

I was born on a day when the good spirits of happiness, long life, honor and wealth hastened to meet me, and my funeral won't lack for high-ranking officials, according to predictions. I haven't caught even a glimpse of the good spirits myself, but a bird flew into the room at the moment of my birth, which my mother considered an auspicious omen. She didn't know what kind of bird it was, but she guessed that it was a small owl. After researching fate, I've come to the conclusion that it works every seventh year. It waits in every person for its moment, like egg cells waiting in a woman, but not every egg cell produces a child. You can prevent your fate from being fulfilled if you live an orderly life, walk along the same streets you've always walked, don't change jobs, stamp your time card, eat and go to sleep at the same time, spend your vacations in the same place, and avoid talking with strangers.

I talked about fate with the Gypsy I met on the Sweden ferry. She was a professional in the field and told me that she had read the future and the past in the Book of Nature. She'd learned to read in Terijoki. For twenty marks she read my palm: in the near future there would be much happiness and great changes in my life. So it was, for three months later I was fired from my job. For free she advised me that I should be more secretive—it isn't necessary to tell everything—because the difficulties that I was having were a result of excessive honesty. Finally she said that my fate would improve at a mature age, as long as I stopped trusting people. Then she moved to the ship's television nook to watch a James Bond video.

There's a rose on the corner of the desk. It smells like a rose, but you don't catch the scent unless you press your nose against the petals. It's yellowish-white in color, like a water lily, and there's a trace of purple at the edges of the petals. Alexander brought it. He said that he'd never seen that sort of rose before and expounded on its qualities. He said that it isn't a rose, it's a symbol. The petals are feelings that wither up and fall off. A five-pointed star remains—that's the person's spirit essence, which never disappears. I'm not sure if I understood him correctly. Last year I received three red roses from him. Is the fading of the color some sort of symbol as well? I straighten the cigarette butts in the ashtray. There are fifty cents in my bank account, there's half a loaf of dry bread on the kitchen table, and in the cupboard there's a potato that reminds me of a whore on Omonia Square. It's just as lonely and wilted. I watched out of the hotel window as she waited the whole long night for customers, leaning against the wall of a side alley, but all the men passed her by. They even want their whores to be young and beautiful, even though it would be more beneficial for their souls if they sinned with an old whore. God would have looked the other way and understood that they did it out of sheer benevolence, in order to assist a poor, ugly woman. She was like any manual laborer whose employer had cast him into the ranks of the unemployed when he became middle-aged. Her professionalism and work experience aren't valued. No one wants to grow up to be a whore or a garbage truck driver, but somebody has to do those jobs, too.

I thought about where I would get money. Should I sell some books to a used bookstore? On the shelf there are two leather-bound copies of *Paradise Lost* that I inherited. People don't read books like that, but I don't have the heart to sell them. Should I start playing the lottery? You can predict racehorses' chances of winning from the stars. A man in France made a prediction and won. He got rich. I don't have the startup capital, and I've even run out of matches too. I lit a candle with the last match. The candle is a thin, brown wax candle, which burns quickly. The Greek Orthodox light them for their saints and their dead. It hisses like there's water mixed in with the wax. Soon there isn't even a stub to set upright, but you can always go get them from bus stops. A friend of mine collects bottles. He's saving up to buy his own apartment.

The sun has come out from behind a cloud and raindrops sparkle on a pine tree when the wind moves the branches.

Alexander gave me a book that advises you to contemplate the fact that the same spirit is in a human being as is in the sun. It elevates the soul. What will happen in my soul if I spend every day thinking about where I can get money for food and to pay the bills? Does the soul gradually become as dry as a ten-mark bill?

{ 10 } The moon just rose from behind the Niemen-mäki tower blocks. It's the size of a frying pan. I'm not young any longer, because I remember old things. I've seen the world's first person to look at the planet from outer space. His name was Yuri Gagarin. He walked past me in a packed classroom, so close that I could have touched him. He was much shorter than I'd imagined from the newspaper pictures. He had fair hair and was wearing a uniform with medals on his breast and a dress hat under his arm. He went behind the teacher's desk and began to talk about what it was like in outer space. "The Earth was beautiful," he said. I don't remember if he said that it was green and blue and much more beautiful than Venus and not a planet of sadness, the way we imagine it. He had an objective conception of the world, because he'd seen it from a distance. We were allowed to ask him questions, but no one dared to ask whether sandwiches and shit float loose in the spaceship. Questions like that interest you when you're a child. I haven't seen any other heroes in my lifetime. But once I saw an angel, even though no one believes it. It didn't have wings, and didn't look like a human being or even an animal. It was more like a large crystal, which reflected the colors of the rainbow and was white at the center. It was higher and wider than the Munkkivuori church steeple. At that time I was a materialist, but I stopped being one when it appeared to me unexpectedly, like some mythical uncle or aunt, who you thought had died a hundred years ago.

At 7:30 the lunar eclipse began. I went to Alexander's place and watched the eclipse through binoculars from his yard. Even the stars are brighter there as long as I'm in love with him. The moon turned dark reddish when the Earth's shadow covered it. It was like a balloon that had escaped from a child. When you grow old there's less and less to wonder about. It doesn't seem surprising anymore that the moon doesn't fall from the sky like a pancake, even though stars are falling all the time.

The dead walk during the full moon, according to old folk wisdom. It's still true, because Father appeared in my dreams that night. He often comes during the full moon. He cooks cabbage soup or makes mushroom gravy. He was a good cook when he was alive, and he hasn't lost his talents where he's resting now. They don't get any newspapers there, and so he comes to earth to find out what's happening. He doesn't frighten me anymore, but when he came for the first time I was scared—he looked so alive. He was wearing a white shirt, but he didn't have a gold crown on his head. He hadn't had time to earn it, because he'd been dead just under a year. He didn't have trousers or a necktie. Maybe in heaven you didn't need them, just a shirt is enough. He sat on the edge of my bed and started to say something. I realized that I was dreaming and that I had to see this dream through to the end, even though I was afraid. At the same moment the room became light: the sun was shining, small gold nuggets glistened on the window curtains, the cat was playing with herring heads on the rug, and Father had disappeared. Mother comes less frequently and doesn't talk with me. She often comes when I intend to make love to some man. She interrupts our intercourse and orders me to do the cleaning or go to the store or take the trash out. When I was young, she gave me permission to go to bed with a man only when I would be able to support myself. I didn't obey her.

Last night, I tried to make love with my father but he ran away from me, terrified. It happened in the summer cabin. I didn't see Mother in the dream. Father fled to the stream; I chased after him. We ran at top speed to the lake, and the water splashed around us. I don't know what would have finally happened there, whether he would have drowned himself like Aino in the *Kalevala*, because I woke up at 2:00. Alexander woke up at the same time. He told me about a long dream, but I only remember that he was drifting on the sea without a rudder, and the wind pushed him to the shore of some unknown land. In the morning he read in Artemidoros's dream book that the sea can be compared to a prostitute, because it first arouses pleasant fantasies, but then treats most people badly. A certain man dreamt he fell into the sea and began to sink. He woke himself up because he was so afraid. The man married a prostitute, moved away with her, and spent most of his life in foreign lands.

My homeland doesn't want me, according to Artemidoros, because intercourse with my father was unsuccessful. I should have moved to some other country twenty years ago, to live under a sky that would be more sympathetic. My head ached. I had drunk too much red wine the night before while watching an American movie about driving from one end of the country to the other in the rain. Nothing else happened in the movie. I didn't have the energy to go home. The sky was blue. The last apple had fallen from its branch during the night. I pressed my stomach and chest against Alexander's back and wound my arm around him. The radio said that Reagan and Gorbachev intend to save the world in December. It will happen in either Vienna or Geneva. By the afternoon I don't remember the morning news anymore. I'm writing this at home. At Alexander's place I'm a guest and I don't do anything. I used to fry pancakes and vacuum, but I stopped when Vera announced that she was going to continue their marriage. In one of the two cities, Reagan and Gorbachev are signing an agreement about the elimination of intermediate-range missiles. It failed in Reykjavik, the news announcer reminded us. The dog flopped down beside me. He smelled like unwashed wool socks and looked me in the eye like a man in love, which Alexander never does. But he isn't in love with me at all, according to him. He dozed off and Artemidoros's dream book fell out of his hands. I picked it up started reading it like a novel.

Artemidoros wrote his book for the poor, for people of low birth and for slaves. Those for whom things are going well don't want explanations of their dreams, but explanations are useful for those who are unlucky in love. There were many unemployed people in the Roman Empire. "Bread and circuses" was the campaign slogan used to fish for their votes. I found out that if a person is nearsighted or if there are thistles between his teeth, or his forehead is bald, it means unemployment. Donkey ears are only good for philosophers. If your hair is long and beautiful, it's a good omen for women, the educated, priests, and prophets. For everyone it signifies wealth. Maybe I'll win the lottery, even though I don't play, because several nights ago my hair was like the hair on Botticelli's *Venus*. I admired myself in the bathroom mirror of my childhood home. But when I tried to cover my vulva with my hair, I noticed that I didn't have one at all——in its place were testicles. If a woman changes into a man it means harder slavery for a slave woman, but it's good for a prostitute, says Artemidoros. Which am I? I wonder on the way home. I came to the conclusion that I'm a prostitute, even though I don't benefit economically from the fact that I bring pleasure to Alexander. On the way it began to rain, and now the rain is so heavy that the trees on the opposite hill have become pale gray.

{ 11 } During the night Anneli fired me from my job. I went to a restaurant, but they weren't serving food. They said that it had run out. I heard somewhere that there was food being offered to the poor at my old school, so I went there. The tables were full of delicacies, but when I reached out my hand someone came to demand payment. He didn't think I wasn't poor enough. I was so hungry that I bellowed in rage and woke myself up. In the morning the frying pan that I inherited from Mother fell off the edge of the sink onto my big toe and cracked. Was it some kind of punishment? Or had an evil Balinese spirit entered into it? They could change into bicycles, cars, kettles and rocks that attacked people. When necessary they change into beautiful young women who turn men's heads so that they begin to act against their own best interests. Sometimes they appear as fireballs and blue flames. A long time ago I met a Balinese person in Amsterdam. I probably wounded his male vanity when I didn't want to make love with him. Maybe he got angry and sent the evil spirit after me, but it didn't know where Finland was and got lost in Siberia, where it wandered around for years causing all sorts of trouble for people. Now it had finally found its destination.

My toe hurts. I sat down on the edge of the bed, unable to decide what I would do. The widow on the upper floor is yelling on the telephone. She has the voice of a market crier. It carries through the ceiling, and I hear that someone pulled down some sheets in the laundry room, the corners are full of dust, and no one takes care of anything in this building, the crows throw trash from the cans into the yard and the leaves that have fallen from the maple trees are pushing into the stairwell, which hasn't been cleaned for two weeks. It sounds like her day has begun badly too. We have a secret soul-connection. We are mirror images of each other and can't stand one another. We know what the world should be like, but the world doesn't oblige us. There is no such thing as justice. If you are fair to one person, you wrong someone else. I've moved the tiger barb out of the aquarium and now it's suffering. It shakes in the corner of the jam jar with its head down and won't eat anything. If I move it back into the aquarium, the angelfish will suffer. Their life together is tragic. The tiger barb nibbles at the angelfish's fins. It enjoys it. It's a sadist. It had an unhappy childhood, too little affection, a mother who ate her children.

Today is again the day when I have to report what I've been doing to the unemployment office. I have no other duties in this society. Five days a week I'm unemployed, but on weekends I have two days off. I go to Alexander's place, drink red wine, watch television, and live like other people. On Monday I return home. The morality of a bureaucrat hangs on tenaciously inside me. If I'm not at the typewriter by eight o'clock, my internal time card begins to flash red, and it feels like the day is being wasted, because I haven't written a single line.

I write the word "unemployed" on the card ten times and the word "weekend" four times. You can't use ditto marks. This resembles my father's method of child rearing. If I'd committed some offence or neglected my duties, I had to write, between ten and fifty times, that a good girl doesn't do things like that. The number depended on how serious my father considered the offense to have been. That's how I learned to be a good girl. I know what I am, because so far I've written almost two hundred times that I'm unemployed. After I've filled out the card and affirmed that to the best of my knowledge the information is accurate, I put it into a brown envelope and go to take it to the unemployment office, which is around the corner.

A neighbor passes me in the yard. He has a small dog; he himself is a large man and doesn't resemble his dog. They still haven't lived together long enough for them to resemble one other, like an old married couple. The man got out of prison a little while ago. He's turned gray and his shoulders have become stooped. He accidentally killed his wife. The wife was a little difficult, drank too much, and sometimes she came to my place hungover to ask me to go to the pharmacy to buy her cough medicine. The man was a good person; he endured and just gritted his teeth the way a Finnish man does when the going gets tough. Perhaps the thought did occur to him sometimes that he could get rid of the old hag. Nothing happens without first existing as a thought in your mind. The man had been cleaning a gun at their summer cabin and was trying it out to see if it worked, when his wife, drunk, had staggered into the path of the bullet. The man's secret wish had been fulfilled. He'd been sentenced to three years, behaved himself well in prison and been freed after one and a half. Now he lives a quiet and solitary life and avoids women.

{ 12 } The earth is dust-colored and there are melancholy puddles in the yard. It's drizzling. Sometimes it feels like being born in Finland is punishment for some sin in a previous life, but when I watch the news on television I think that maybe my birth wasn't so bad after all, since I wasn't born in Palestine or Siberia. During the night I applied for a job at the Leningrad harbor. There was a long line in front of the office. A rumor had been going around town that anyone could get a job there and they weren't checking papers. There were lots of people in line who had been in exile or in prison camps. My turn came. The hiring officer was a man who looked at me appraisingly and said that I could have a job if I'd give it up to him. I slapped him on the cheek and marched out of the office, furious. After me came a thin professor who hadn't gotten a job either. Maybe he was one of the travelers headed for Moscow, whom I had happened to look at while I was walking through the station. The *Leo Tolstoy* was standing next to the platform and smelled good, like the trains when I was a child.

I was coming from an interview arranged by the employment service and it felt like I had failed. Two men sat behind a long table and interrogated me. One was dark and slim, he had long pianist's fingers and a cream-colored suit, the other was an ordinary, quiet man. They offered me coffee in paper cups and told me that the work was taking care of circulating shared journal subscriptions and copying scientific articles.

"Is a university degree required for that?" I asked in surprise.

The dark one thought that one was, because it was demanding work. The quiet one asked whether I knew chemistry.

"I remember the formula for oxygen, but not for nitrogen. I got a D in that subject."

The dark one asked if I drank, did I get along well with co-workers, what sort of family relationships I had, did I intended to get married, have children, or move away from the area in the near future.

"What do you do outside of working hours?" asked the quiet one.

"Write and read."

I didn't tell them about the dream interpretation and astrology so that I wouldn't give a strange picture of myself. Maybe I should have said squash and sailing, because I think that they were looking at me strangely.

I looked like Don Quixote's horse when I saw myself in the department store mirror after the interview. There was a run in my stocking, my jacket hung like an empty sack and my cheeks were hollow. They won't give me that job, I thought, and I don't want it, either. I still haven't written about my childhood and youth. I haven't gotten any farther than the beginning. I made a face at the image in the mirror. Not at myself, but at the man who sits behind the mirror looking at women. Department store mirrors lie. They're made of special glass that affects women's eyes so they'll buy a new dress or maybe just lipstick. The women don't know that behind the mirror there's a booth and that it's a man's job to sit there. He's paid to catch thieves. Every morning he opens a little door and goes inside the pillar that the mirror is attached to. Gradually he goes stir-crazy and can't stand to be anywhere at home but in the closet. He sits there and berates his wife. A friend of mine married a detective but divorced him after two years, because he just interrogated her all night long. She wouldn't acknowledge that she was guilty of anything and the man became more and more violent.

My right palm itches and my hair is tangled. The brush and comb have disappeared. A fire truck goes by the window. It's noisy and moves slowly. A flock of small birds flutters down to sit on the branches of the pine tree. They have yellow on their breasts. They aren't blue tits—maybe they're yellowhammers. In the bird book it says that the yellowhammer, a silent and modest fellow, doesn't attract much attention, and so has remained unknown to the public at large. By its nature it is quiet and serious and its song is melancholy. Am I a former yellowhammer? When autumn comes I always have this desire to leave the country. It's written in the stars that I won't achieve any success in my native land. I'll find happiness far from home, among people I don't know. A good friend of mine says that people have free will. If that's so, a person can prevent his fate from being fulfilled. With willpower you'll surely succeed. If I weren't poor, I would travel by train to Brindisi. I've never been there and train trips enchant me. You meet interesting people on them, but the sorts of things that happen in books never happen to me. That love flares instantly between an unknown woman and man and they go to the restroom to make love. I don't see how that could work in such a cramped, swaying place. Maybe it's easy for the small and supple. I'm so slow that I don't even notice the possibilities before the trip is over. The last time I traveled across Europe, a Yugoslavian shoemaker was taken with my shoes. He stroked them tenderly and asked where they were from. I said from Finland.

"Let's get married; I have a beautiful house on the coast of the Adriatic Sea," he said to the shoes.

But the shoes gave the shoemaker his walking papers. He didn't take it badly, but gave me his address, if I happened to change my mind after I got back to Finland. On the train to Milan, I met a castle owner named Giovanni, Jussi in Finnish. All the men that I've fallen in love with in my life have been Jussis. Alexander is a Jussi too. The castle was near Merano and he asked me to come there, but I didn't go with him, because he had frayed sleeve cuffs, a dirty shirt collar and unshaved stubble, and I didn't believe in his castle. Perhaps it was a cloud castle. I have expensive tastes, Mother said long ago.

{ 13 } Now I've changed into a man completely. I walk through the village and drag behind me a bundle of twigs. The village is full of brown-shirted soldiers. They order the people to their knees. People have to obey them, otherwise the soldiers will shoot, but I don't participate in the subservience. I'm so crazy that I get to do what I want. My actions don't have any significance. I go to the church hill and meet a little old woman who is standing on the steps of her cottage. She tells me about the living and the dead and asks me into the cottage for coffee, but I don't have time. I have to go where I'm going. Two soldiers open a gate for me, which is in front of the road leading to the shore. They laugh at me, because I'm the village lunatic and you're supposed to laugh at someone like that, otherwise you're not a man or something.

"What are you going to do there?" asks one.

I shrug my shoulders; I say, "Nothing much."

"There isn't space. There's a fleet assembling there and lots of people moving around," says the other.

I go anyway. From far away I look at the blue sea and the white sandy shore. I don't have any business being here, I think, and leave.

Again I see the little old woman. She's walking along the edge of the field, leading a cow. In the field there are people stooping down toward the ground and smoke is rising into the air. I'm on West Street, and I search for Alexander's building between the Swedish school and my old building, but I don't find it and get upset like a child who's gotten lost. I'm looking for his house in the wrong direction. It isn't in the south, where I've come from. I've lost the key and I don't know where to go. In big cities, the stations are open at night, but Helsinki isn't a big city. I'm cold, tired, I start to become desperate. I have to get somewhere to rest and warm up. On Huopalahti Road I notice I have a silver chain around my neck and the key to my old house is hanging there. I creep in silently, so that I don't wake up the current occupants. I go to the toilet and curl up on the floor in a ball, like a cat. I fall asleep.

Do I have to go back there? I wondered in the morning. Why do the dreams take me back there? I've visited that bathroom twice in one week. In English, they say that there's a skeleton in the closet when something is hidden in the past.

When I think about my youth, in my mind it's always evening or night, freezing, there's wind blowing from the sea toward my face and the air is full of small pricking thorns. Maybe I have to go back some day. It's quite close to here, barely a kilometer away. I haven't been there for ten years. I've walked along Stockholm's Kungsgatan more often than West Street.

For some reason I feel revulsion towards the past. I'm reminded of the story about Jesus and his disciples, who saw the carcass of a dead dog by the side of the road.

"Yuk, it's so ugly," said the disciples and went by quickly. But Jesus stopped to look, and said:

"It has beautiful white teeth. They glisten like mother-of-pearl."

{ 14 } On Father's Day I walked from one end to the other of a road that I call West Street, but which no longer has that name on the map. Flags hung limply on their flagpoles. When Father turned fifty, the building super wouldn't agree to put up the flag, even though Father was an important person. He'd seen the Tsar's daughters swimming, received medals and shaken hands with Mannerheim. The super didn't think this was anything special. Behind the red brick school building old black alders lined the road, but the pines had died, only the dead tree trunks were left, and the Gypsies' house had been demolished. Not even the foundation stones were left. As I was walking from north to south, my face toward the past and my back to the future, I thought that I'm like a crayfish that scurries backward into a rock crevice. I turned to the left and walked along the north side of Park Road past the Primula where I used to sit and smoke after school, until I was banned for the next thirty years. I don't remember what I said to the manager of the cafeteria, but she got angry. When I was young, adults got annoyed with me easily. I didn't even need to say anything for them to explode. The principal's neck swelled up and his face turned red when I laughed in the middle of history class. He pointed to the door and shouted, "You're laughing at me. Get out!"

On the gray electrical box fastened to the wall of the Primula building was written, "This is a sad story. This story is true." Boys don't write things like that. Some girl that was raped by her father, I thought, because Alexander's daughters had told me that it's surprisingly common nowadays. They knew of several cases. They said that their father at least had his good side: he'd never tried anything with them. He seemed to me like a fairly tolerable father. He even talks with his daughters. Some time ago he said to his younger daughter that she should choose one or the other of her two boyfriends, because it isn't right to date two at the same time.

"And what about you? You have two women," I teased him.

"That's different," he said.

He looked like all honorable and honest men do when a woman points out to them that they don't live according to their ideals and teachings, something they know perfectly well themselves. Their faces turn sheepish, their eyes start to wander along the floor and they don't seem to know how to hold their mouths. It clams shut and their ears go back. Then they clear their throats and change the subject.

I went across Park Road and walked along its south side. I thought that even in this well-to-do part of the city some father is raping his daughter. My surgeon friend Vasily was dancing, high as a kite, between the linden trees and roaring at passersby. I turned onto West Street. In front of my building the poplars had grown as high as the fifth floor. They reached toward the sky like thin candle flames. A few leaves hung on the branches, which smelled like used sauna whisks. A young father came by pushing a baby carriage. He had a blond ponytail and a gold ring in his ear. He turned onto Park. There was no sign of the mother. She'd probably gone for a beer with her girlfriends. Fathers used to be different. You were supposed to be afraid of and respect them, and their word was law. If it was necessary, they gave you a beating. They'd been in the war and saved Finland. They ate and read the newspaper and you weren't allowed to bother them. They growled if you said anything to them. They had brown briefcases that they took papers out of and spread out on the desk after their afternoon rest. In the morning they went with the briefcase to the streetcar or to a black car and drove into town, where they made important decisions. Finland's economy, well-being, and future depended on them. They were much older than fathers today, who are virtually children.

{ 15 } Making progress on paper is slow. Evening and night pass before the trip ends. All kinds of things happen that interrupt writing. The telephone rings: Alexander is depressed; an acquaintance drops by and a neighbor comes to borrow some cardamom; there's a TV show I have to watch. Reagan has threatened to attack Iran and the stock markets have crashed around the world. In the night I was running from Mother along Park Road. I'd gone to the kiosk to buy the morning paper and ran away so that she wouldn't take it away from me. When she was alive she always wanted to be the first to read the paper. I ran to the cellar of a plumbing company's building where I was living and pulled the curtains across the window. It was so dark that I don't think she saw me. In my dreams I don't like her; she disturbs my life and I don't want to see her. She's something within me that appears in Mother's guise. The picture we get of our parents doesn't have anything to do with reality.

Yesterday I stood in the backyard of my old building. It was deserted and silent. Sparrows chirped in the hedge and a yellow plastic crocodile lay in the sand box. I glanced at the fourth floor to see if the big-headed, buzzard-like man was still sitting by the window reading old, black-covered books that looked like the Bible. He wasn't anybody's father or husband. He lived the solitary life of an old bachelor, didn't go outside and didn't like children or the women who beat rugs on the balcony next to his window. He glared at them angrily, but his look didn't have any effect. Had he chosen solitude voluntarily or had it just happened to him like winning a lottery? There was no sign of him. Maybe he'd died or moved to the sort of building where there weren't any women banging on carpets.

I continued my way south on West Street and thought about whether I'm old enough to write about youth. It didn't feel like it. I passed the Swedish school where Alexander had gone for a couple of grades. Since he had been from a family that was poorer than that of the school's other pupils, he'd been teased constantly, and it left bitter memories. As an adult he'd joined the Finnish Alliance and started to oppose the Swedes. I didn't have anything against them, because when I was six years old, I fell in love with a boy from the Swedish school who said he was the emperor of China. He was twice my age, but love is blind to age, time, and place. Ninon de l'Enclos was ninety years old when a man half her age fell passionately in love with her. She'd been the mistress of hundreds of men and she was still an attractive woman even when she was old.

On the corner of West and Cadet Street, just past the Swedish school, is the building where I was conceived and lived my first years. I remembered it as white, but it was light brown. I learned to walk and talk there. My first sentence revealed what kind of character I would have. With perfect grammar I said: "That is my stack," and pointed to the biggest stack of pancakes on the serving tray. Before that I hadn't spoken a word. My favorite book was Rabelais's *Gargantua*, which I studied so thoroughly as a child that the binding cracked and many of the pages fell out. Gargantua was a glutton and wine-drinker whose soul was in the kitchen. I thought it was especially amusing that he ate pilgrims with salad, wiped his backside with a goose, and pissed from the steeple of Notre Dame.

Taste and smell were first in my world, then came color. I remember the sweet taste of mashed potatoes and rose-hip sauce and the smell of Mother's powder, which got into my nose and made me sneeze. I don't have very many memories of my first house, but I remember the yellow color, which there was so much of that it dazzled the eyes. I remember a child as tall as a dandelion who blew fuzz into the air at the edge of a field. The field was visible from the window of my house and beyond the field was the blue sea. People squatted on their pieces of land and smoke climbed into the air. The name of the place was Ox Pasture, but I never saw any oxen there. There isn't any field anymore. It's been made into a park, and in the middle of the park is a pond where ducks and some black birds were swimming around. I walked toward the sea. I could see it gray at the end of the road. On the left side of the road was a red brick tower. It used to be a mill; now some designer lives there. It's the tower where I've locked up Mother in my imagination.

I stood on the shore and looked at the sea. I was disappointed because this childhood landscape didn't fit my mental images, in which everything was much more open, sunny, and brighter than in reality. What I was searching for wasn't on West Street. Ultimately, I don't know what I was searching for and why the dreams took me to that road even though there wasn't anything there. As I stood there, the sun emerged from the fog. Around the sun was a dark ring bordered by a rainbow. I had never seen the sun like that in a puddle before.

{ 16 } I'm reading the newspaper and humming, "No more pencils, no more books, no more teachers' dirty looks." Cardinal Jaime Sin from the Philippines says, "When you're hungry, you see visions," and encourages people to eat properly so that the visions will stop. He's concerned that the Virgin Mary has begun to appear outside the church hierarchy, to the common people, who don't understand the finer points of dogma and misinterpret the Virgin's pronouncements about the world's political situation. I'm eating burned wheat porridge when Liisa S.'s face comes to mind. Is she thinking of me? She'll probably call soon and ask me how I'm getting along. It often happens that a person appears first in your thoughts and then calls. In Lapland it's called a false arrival. Liisa S. was a classmate of mine, but she didn't graduate. Unhappy love affairs took up her time. She was one of the rare people who still believed in the socialist revolution. Her faith was the only stable feature in her. Everything else was flickering, uncertain and desperate. I met her one day at the bus stop. She was coming from a meeting, looking tired, and told me that she'd only slept one hour last night. Black circles under her eyes and red streaks on her neck as though she'd scratched herself in agony. She took hold of my arm. She always had to touch the person she was talking with. For my part, I didn't like being touched unnecessarily. She leaned on my arm confidingly and whispered in my ear that I mustn't tell anyone, but that she was seeing a married man.

"They all have back-up women at home," she said with a bitter tone in her voice.

The bus came, and I didn't have time to console her that there are good things about it too. She can be a pleasure and comfort for the man, but she doesn't have the unpleasant responsibilities of a wife. Many women no doubt envy her, for leading the free and mysterious life of a mistress. She's my companion in fate. My brother said there wasn't any wife in me. Brothers and sisters will always tell you the truth if you don't happen to know it otherwise. But there's no point believing Gypsies. One Gypsy told me in front of the National Museum that I had the signs of a happy marriage on my palm. Knowing that cost ten marks. I'd just gotten engaged, but I didn't dare get married. I was afraid of a final commitment and I guess I'm still afraid, because my relationship with Alexander is temporary (like all my jobs have been too). When Vera comes, I'll leave. It's like a changing of the guard.

I was disappointed and enraged when Alexander told me that Vera wants to continue their marriage, but he still won't discard me, even though he still loves Vera and waits for the day when Vera will come to Finland. He said that life is a game and we're the pieces higher powers play with. I said that I'm no game piece, that I'm not participating in any game, collected my things into two plastic bags and left so definitively that I don't even have a toothbrush over there now. When he said that he doesn't intend to divorce Vera, the watch that he'd given me as a present broke, the numbers disappeared suddenly and they haven't come back even though I bought a new battery. Nearly a year has passed since then. I can tell the passage of time from the striking of the neighbor's clock. From the increasing or diminishing of the light, I know when it's morning or evening. When I hear the stroke of twelve o'clock on the radio, I know that it's midday. I see what the name of the day is in the newspaper. Today is Wednesday, the day of Mercury, dedicated to merchants and thieves. Today I have to make a report of my activities to the unemployment office.

{ 17 } I went to the beach to walk after the mail came and brought a letter that said, "In order to place you in a civil service position, we request that you come to the employment office, Higher Education Department, or call 902-2409." I didn't call, and I didn't go to the office. I'm made up of work-resistant material. Last week I didn't get in touch with the school administration inspection office, which had submitted an order for a civil service employee. I thought: I'm not an object that can be ordered. A person has the right to choose what she does. I'd rather become a tube of toothpaste than a civil servant.

"Dear employer, during my lifetime I've managed to do a great deal, but I haven't been a tube of toothpaste yet. I've delivered newspapers, sorted vegetables, built stone walls, taught Swedish and English, counted money orders, weighed parcels, taken care of lunatics, sold patterns and sewing machine needles, downloaded medical reports from diskettes, organized archives, corresponded with Ugandan and South African statistics officials, written minutes of meetings, gathered information and made history."

Nowadays, I live the lifestyle of the future. In the future people will no longer need to go to work and money will become meaningless. In the newspaper two unemployed people expressed their pleasure that they had the chance to use their time as they saw fit. They admitted that they enjoyed life and were satisfied living off unemployment. They shouldn't have said that. A mass of indignant citizens replied to them; they were of the opinion that it is irresponsible to enjoy life. An unemployed person is supposed to suffer and drink booze, engage in drunken brawls, and finally commit suicide. The happy unemployed shake society's foundations and gnaw at the nation's moral backbone. The future is close, I thought, as I walked. The stock markets have collapsed and the exchange rate of the dollar drops every day. A natural remedy has been developed in California called St. John's Cure. It helps if your faith in God begins to waver, or if you have difficulties with your father.

At the beach a little, chubby child came toward me, looking serious. Walking was new to him and he had to concentrate on it. The child's grandmother exchanged a few words with me. She remarked that the weather was warm, even though it was already November and that last summer in Ostrobothnia there hadn't been a single day as warm as this. I thought that old people are no longer shy about life or about people, either, but talk with strangers as though they were acquaintances.

It was midday, the rocks and trees cast long shadows. The sun was shining at an angle across the bay. I went to sit at the base of that pine where I always sit. A wasp flew sluggishly onto my knee and stayed there to warm itself. By my feet lay a shoe named Peter Black, from Great Britain. Among shoes from which owners have exited, worn-out slippers seem the most orphaned. They long for feet to warm them. Someone had built a fire between the rocks and eaten a liver casserole and smoked some Guild pipe tobacco. The girl I'd seen on the shore on Saturday and Sunday hadn't come today. She sat behind a stone, but I could see her dark hair and shoulders, which were hunched humbly as though she were praying. She sat in the same position for so long that my curiosity was aroused; I thought that no one could pray so long and so devoutly, especially not a young person. I walked past her to see what she was doing. She was writing in a Chinese notebook, which had black covers with red corners. She was overcome by inspiration and didn't notice me. She wrote without raising her eyes or lifting the pen from the paper. Was she unburdening her heart? Was she writing about love? What other subject does a young woman have to write about when she doesn't know about death yet? I thought she was such a beautiful girl that things would go badly for her. Some man will fall in love with her and want her for his own; she'll fly into the cage and stop writing. She had an engagement ring—things had already gone wrong for her. Her fiancé laughs strangely when she says she writes, becomes jealous and starts to pick at her cruelly. The girl feels guilty—she doesn't want to cause distress for anyone—and starts to write in secret; she comes to the beach whenever her fiancé won't notice. They get married, have children and the girl doesn't write anymore.

When she turns ninety, she'll be interviewed on television. They'll ask why she stopped writing, even though she was a gifted poet when she was young. She says, "My husband was so jealous of me."

She's so old that she's no longer bitter and doesn't hold it against her husband. She giggles like a young girl at the interviewer, who's a man.

Some man was standing in the thicket and staring at me like a cat whose face reveals what it's planning. He didn't know that I'm not a woman when I'm writing. I'm not a man either—I'm Mercury, who has no gender. I left, because I don't like having someone standing behind me staring. It reminds me of my school days and the teacher's squeaky shoes when she crept between the desks, watching to see that no one cheated during exams. The man standing in the thicket wasn't dangerous, just an ordinary exhibitionist. I've never met a rapist in my life, except once in Sibelius Park, but I'm not sure whether he was a real rapist: he took off when I bit his hand. I was fifteen years old, big and strong, and I had front teeth like a hare. I guess that rapists think that it isn't worthwhile to attack a woman with such large teeth. When my teeth fall out, my bones become brittle, and I can't run away, I'll start being afraid of them.

{ **18** } It's gray and misty, like Central Europe in the winter. From the window I can see the first of twelve telephone poles. On the other side of the street is a pile of chopped poplars. They're greenish-gray. A little farther away there's a pole with a notice about forestry maintenance. My eyes can't see that far, but I went to see what it said on my way back from Alexander's place. It's good when people are notified about what's going on, so they don't worry, I thought. Now I'm grieving over the fallen trees as though they were lost friends. My heart is knotted up and things fall out of my hands all day. A glass of milk crashed to the floor and shattered, a knife escaped under the table, and I sat down on a frying pan with spaghetti sauce in it. I'd left it on my chair. Dreams confuse my feelings. During the night I participated in a swimming competition and came in first in the ten thousand meter race, but the judges didn't certify the result; instead they announced that the winner was a woman who'd come to the finish line after me and only swam three thousand meters. I argued with the judges, because I thought their decision was unfair, but they clung to their contention that the other one was better, even though she swam diagonally across the pool, breaking all the rules. When I woke up I knew that it was Vera. The three thousand meters meant the three years she'd been married to Alexander. Last week was their anniversary. I wouldn't have known, but there was a three-year-old almanac page of the name-day for "Panu" fastened with a pin to the side of the bookshelf.

"You have a wife, but she isn't much of life companion. She doesn't share your life, just your money," I told Alexander, but he didn't like that.

He furrowed his brow, and I was afraid that he'd leave me. He didn't, but he was between a rock and a hard place. He said, "Let's give it some time."

When I told him about the swimming dream, it touched a nerve, and he said that I'm the sort of person who has to invent suffering, even in dreams, if there isn't any around.

"The next night you'll probably have a dream about swimming fifty kilometers," he said.

A book fell from his shelf in the morning, opening to the passage that said, "A thousand reasons to worry, a thousand reasons to be shy—they bind the fool, not the wise man." He lifted the book from the floor onto the edge of the shelf and said that that sentence was for me. It was Indian wisdom, but it didn't make me a single bit wiser. I called him a fool, felt guilty afterward, and made morning coffee for him even though I don't usually do that.

{ **19** } A man is talking on the radio in a tender voice, like that of a pigeon cooing. He is describing how he meets people in his work who drain his strength. In his free time he collects old dictionaries of foreign words and phrases. He thinks that language ought to be protected because it's so easily damaged. I can't figure out what his profession is. Based on his voice, I'd wager he's a priest, but what he says points to his being a psychiatrist, because he says that fundamentally women don't yearn for freedom but for fulfillment. I feel a twinge when he uses the expression "a functioning relationship." Some committee of bureaucrats probably invented it. It brings to mind the summer cabin's red electric pump. When you pressed the button, it started to whir and pump water into the sauna. As it aged, it became bad-tempered and stubborn, as old people often do. It went on strike and only worked when it felt like it. I'm jealous, because I don't have a functioning relationship, and I lost the pump along with the cabin. I have a three-way relationship, but it doesn't function properly, because I can't stand competition. I'm a poor loser. If it looks like I'm starting to lose, I don't bother to play anymore. I'm like that trotting horse that went to the green to eat grass in the middle of the race. I had bet on that horse and lost my money, about twenty marks, no more than that. After seeing it in the program, I though it was a beautiful horse, because it had a star on its forehead and the legs of a runner.

My back and neck hurt—they hurt in the morning when I woke up—and I'm in a foul mood. An angry female ghost was jumping up and down on my neck and I couldn't do anything about it. It disturbed my sleep. It was a reflection of my thoughts. It was Vera. Before I fell asleep, I thought that she's in this story merely to torment me, in order to create suspense. You can expect all sorts of twists and turns from her. Alexander considers her a rare person because he sees himself in her; one of my acquaintances who met her says she's crazy, and Alexander's daughter says she's a gold-digger. I think she's a liar. I began to suspect that she lies without the slightest hesitation when she said once that in her country private citizens aren't allowed to own cameras. I knew that it wasn't true. Truth and lies are so tightly intertwined in her speech that they're impossible to seperate. I doubt she can tell them apart herself. She's an educated person—attended university, finished a law degree—and was in a well-paid position in some government office. She says she's sacrificed her profession and social position for her love of Alexander; because of him she had to give up her position and hasn't found a new job, since she's married to a foreigner. It sounded so pathetic that it was hard to believe that it was true. Maybe half was true. Of course it could have been mere coincidence that Vera fell in love and got married at the same time as her office was under investigation for corruption and many civil servants had to leave—some voluntarily, some against their will. Fate sent Alexander there at just the right time—Vera fell head over heels when she saw him and proposed to him within a half-hour of meeting.

Alexander described the proposal "As though the ceiling had fallen on my head." "You couldn't have been in your right mind then," I said.

He wouldn't admit that it appealed to his vanity to have a beautiful woman propose to him. He said that it was a matter of life and death. I started to feel that he'd met with a serious accident, which he hadn't survived. He was living in the grip of some strange obsession.

Perhaps Vera's love had been genuine as long as it had lasted. But soon after the marriage, faults started to appear in Alexander that she hadn't noticed while she was infatuated. It often goes that way. At first the faults are minor, but irritating. A man snores and smells of sweat. He dresses badly, his trousers sag, his socks are worn out and his pockets hang down like a farmer's. He has no table manners. He eats like a pig and doesn't wash his hands before coming to the table. Your girlfriends look down on him; your father criticizes you for ending up with someone like him, even though you could have had any man in *this* country. And your mother weeps, nags and is ashamed to show her face. Vera's hopes all ended in disappointment. She wanted a Western car, a fur coat, and a Visa card, but didn't get them. Alexander brought her his ex's clothes and a black umbrella, even though he was supposed to bring her Italian shoes and Dior blouses. Vera started to call him a pig, a pig who couldn't appreciate her feelings and didn't know how to treat a sophisticated woman, because he was used to dating Neanderthals. She didn't want to see Alexander anymore, demanded a divorce and ten thousand marks as alimony, but she changed her mind a few months later and explained that she hadn't meant what she said. It was all the fault of a certain witch whom she had given power over her and who had ruined her marriage. I didn't believe that story.

It's been some time since the witches in her country followed their victims around and imitated their movements. They were able to bewitch their victims by identifying with them. It created a feeling of sympathy, which the victim couldn't perceive. When the witch tripped, the victim tripped. Nothing happened to the sorcerer, but the victim broke her leg, hit her head, or something else crazy happened. That's where the saying "To weave plots behind someone's back" comes from. Nowadays that sort of thing doesn't happen, but in some outlying villages there are still women who can heal the sick and create infatuations using magical powers. One old woman murmured incantations into a bottle with tea in it. When the patient drank the tea or rubbed a sore place with it, he got better. She was also known as a skilled healer of children's rashes. She intrigued me because she happened to live in my grandparents' old house. I wanted to meet her, but she wouldn't let me in because I was a foreigner. Maybe she was afraid she'd get into trouble because of me. I haven't heard of any other witches, but sometimes I've seen half-grown girls walking behind grown women imitating their movements and gestures exaggeratedly, snickering maliciously the whole time. And sometimes lovebirds start to mimic each other, but because they don't do it with any evil intent, it isn't witchcraft, just enchantment, and it probably happens everywhere in the world.

{ 20 } I often used to look at Vera's picture, which was attached to the side of the bookshelf. The picture was shriveled and had turned a reddish brown. One evening it fell down and Alexander didn't fasten it back onto the side of the bookshelf. Vera had the same look as Mother. Dark bangs, eyes, and eyebrows like Mother had, but Vera's lips were thin and her expression sterner. She looked like she knew what she wanted. In the picture she was bent over resolutely signing the marriage certificate. She had a slender wrist and held the pen neatly in her hand. I don't know if I'd like her if I knew her, but I'm sure that in reality she's a person quite different from Snow White's step-mother, the way she appears in my dreams and imagination.

Long ago she was a little girl in the town of Ivanovo. She had large silken bows in her hair and drew pictures of princesses like all little girls, no matter whether they lived in a capitalist country or a socialist country. She sucked her finger shyly, lifted up the hem of her skirt and clung to her father's or grandfather's side, longing for affection. If someone spoke a harsh word to her, tears came to her eyes, and her lips began to tremble. Then she went to school and learned to lie and disguise her feelings. You had to learn those skills if you wanted to succeed and live long in the world. She learned that there was the official truth, which no one believed, but which you had to pretend to believe, and then there was the other truth, which you couldn't talk about out loud. Her parents whispered mysteriously, but when she asked what they were saying, their faces went stiff and they pretended not to know what she was talking about. Vera grew up and her parents' secrets stopped interesting her. She started going to her girlfriends' houses, learned to dance, to walk in high-heeled shoes and paint her lips. In the evenings she walked arm in arm with Rosa and Lilya along Ivanovo's boardwalks, humming Beatles tunes that were popular at the time. When some pleasant boy came toward her, she giggled, making the boy's ears turn red. She practiced looking at boys out of the corner of her eye like adult women did, and didn't giggle anymore, instead gliding past them haughtily and casting a quick look at them from the shadow of her eyelashes. She read Anna Akhmatova's love poems, because they weren't read in school, detested Mayakovsky, because he was required reading, and was later infatuated with Kostya, Vitya, or Dimka, but secretly she daydreamed about a great and fateful love, like Anna Karenina's love affair, but without the tragic ending. She went to the capital city to study, met Volodya, fell in love and got pregnant. She got married at nineteen, had a daughter, graduated at twenty-three, did two years of compulsory work in a small Siberian town as a public prosecutor's assistant, and then moved back to the capital. Her uncle, a three-star general, arranged a government job for her and an apartment near the center of town, on Melnikova Street. Within a year she was already disappointed in the marriage. Volodya turned out to be a good-for-nothing, was selfish and lazy, drank, behaved like a savage in bed, and cheated on her with a village girl. She got divorced and decided that she'd never get married again, at least not to a Russian man. Her girlfriend Marina had married an American and gotten everything that Vera dreamed of. And with the alimony after the divorce, she didn't need to go to work. She dedicated herself to artistic pursuits, whose precise nature I don't know. Vera raised her daughter, went to work, and advanced in her job, acquiring subordinates and a better salary. Her life was in order, but it lacked freedom and love; she wasn't satisfied, even though she was always infatuated with some Yuri, Vasily, or Nikolai, and they with her. Yuri painted pictures, Vasily was an actor, and Nikolai did magic tricks in the circus. But there was always some fault in each. Vera gave up on them and wrote a book about God. It wasn't published in her country and she sent the manuscript to New York, but never heard anything back. When she turned thirty-five, some typist in her office saw in the cards that a blond man would come from far away and she would get married. And so she did. After a year she met Alexander in a studio on Arbat Street.

Last summer I visited Melnikova Street. I had Vera's telephone number, but didn't dare call her and I thought that I'd go and see what kind of building she lives in. I took the subway there and planned the way that I would ring her doorbell, say that

I was from Finland, and that I'd come to see Faina Panova, a friend of mine. Vera says that nobody by that name lives at this address. She goes to close the door; I explain anxiously that I don't know what to do, I'm probably lost, since the buildings look so much alike, and ask her if I can telephone Faina Panova from her place. Vera lets me in, because I'm a Finn, and they are an honest, albeit simple people. I call Faina, who isn't home. I know that she left in the morning to do some official business, and that takes time. I scratch my head as though in doubt, sit on a chair in the same room and Vera doesn't know what to do with me. She's confused. She's not so old that she would offer tea. In Russia the old women are glad to serve tea. They don't do it out of good will but out of curiosity, because they want to know the stranger's business, where she came from, and where she's going. The stranger will give her enough to gossip about all day. I asked her if she knows Vera Ramenskaya. She's startled because the question was so unexpected. She glances at me suspiciously, but doesn't show her cards; she asks, feigning indifference, "What about her?" I say that she's the wife of a friend of mine, but how can she love my friend, because she promises to come but never does, just inventing excuses. She probably married for money, not for love. Vera pales visibly.

At this stage my plan began to resemble Natasya Filippovna and Aglaia Ivanovna's famous meeting in *The Idiot*, which ends with one fainting and the other running away. They loved the same man. I didn't have time to develop a different ending, because the subway came to my stop. I walked along Melnikova Street, which had a grocery store, a bookstore, an interior decorating shop, and an ice cream and beer stand on it. Melnikova was some heroine, presumably a partisan who killed Germans and was killed herself. Her street was shaded by linden trees, under which flourished a mass of weeds, as in all Russian parks. The lilacs were fragrant; they'd just started to blossom. I found block number five, but not building number two, where Vera lived. I walked around and looked at the area. Jackdaws were screeching, thin cats crept through the bushes in the yard, and from somewhere far away I could hear the sounds of children playing. The buildings were constructed of gray prefab concrete slabs and reminded me of the buildings in Munich's Uterhacking, with the difference that the balconies there weren't piled with junk. I didn't see any old women dressed in black. They usually sit on the benches in the yard, gossiping. They'd probably changed into jackdaws and flown into the trees to squawk at each other. An old man who looked like a country yokel was marveling at a sparrow that was pecking with its beak on the side window of a Lada and peeping now and then at the rearview mirror.

"What a conceited bird. I've never seen anything like it," said the man.

"Neither have I," I said.

The man looked at me for a long time.

"I'm a foreigner," I explained with my bad pronunciation.

"Excuse me," the man said and lifted his cap.

I'd already given up looking for Vera's building and was about to leave when a slight breath of wind came and swept aside the lilac branches from the wall of the building I was walking past, revealing the number two. It seemed as though the

Russian house-gnome had been playing tricks on me. At first he didn't want to show me Vera's building, but at the last minute he changed his mind. I'd gone past it three or four times, but I hadn't noticed it because it was attached to building number one so they were almost the same building. I stood in front of the entrance; two schoolboys and a limping mixed-breed dog went in. I could have gone in after them and asked where Ramenskaya lived, but I didn't go and didn't ask. It began to drizzle. I turned and was leaving for the subway station when a stylish woman in Western clothes walked past me near the corner of the building. She had white, high-heeled boots, an English raincoat, and a blue-checked umbrella. I was a bit startled and looked closely at her. Was she Vera? Her face was oval and her chin was narrow, like in the wedding picture, but she didn't have bangs. Her hair was short and rose up from her forehead in the current fashion. I'd also seen a picture of her where her hair was cropped close to her head and there was an expression of suffering on her face. She'd looked like someone who escaped from prison. The woman who went past me was self-confident and conscious of her beauty. A woman who looks like that doesn't get depressed about little things. I thought if she was Vera, she would look down her nose at me and think, "Who does that buffoon think she is?" I decided to invite Vera to the Baku restaurant to eat and talk things over. After I got to my hotel I telephoned her. Her daughter answered the phone and said she'd gone to the countryside for a couple of days. When she heard my name, she asked whether Alexander was in town too. I said he wasn't and asked her to have her mother call me back. Vera didn't call.

{ 21 } The world has been saved again. The people who did it were standing side by side on the television, telling jokes and smiling, pleased with themselves. Our lives haven't been spent in vain—they'd signed a treaty about the destruction of medium-range missiles in countries they didn't even run. The event was broadcast live last night. I suspected they were just acting. Wars are caused by the leaders of great powers entering into agreements among themselves. During the night I dreamed that Mannerheim was being buried. I wondered which Mannerheim was the real one, the one that died long ago, or this one whose funeral the people were lined up for on Mechelin Street. When I woke up, I thought that heroes die twice. First the body dies and then the glory. Margaret Thatcher cooed happily on television that the new treaty was the finest Christmas present that the world could have received. I am following the footsteps of these statesmen. Last spring I followed Thatcher to Zagorsk and Jacques Chirac to Pasternak's grave. Chirac's flowers hadn't had time to wither. Thatcher reminded me that the yearly disruption is approaching.

Once again I will be forced to face my childhood traumas; this is always a depressing time for me. How do children feel about their mother running away with Santa Claus? They probably continue the tradition as adults, because people have a tendency to repeat what they experience during childhood.

The Edda poems say that all the grief of a person's life comes to mind early in the morning. The moon is leaning against the chimney of the building next door, his hands in his pockets and his shoulders slouched. He's been fired from his job and doesn't know where to go. He's thin; his stomach is hollow. He hasn't eaten properly for two weeks. He pulls his cap down over his eyes and slinks behind the chimney.

The skins of some passion fruits are on the table. They smell like winos and cat's piss. In some languages suffering and passion are the same word. Some man who had suffered a great deal because of love picked the fruit up from the ground and turned it over in his hand, wondering what it was, since it was so wrinkled and had such an ugly color. He pressed it with his thumb and it yielded, feeling soft inside. He split it open and saw that inside there was a yellowish-white, slimy substance, like frogspawn, and the seeds were black, like sorrow or anger. Sticky liquid oozed onto his fingers. He tried it and it tasted good. He took it to his woman as a present, because he was such a poor man that he didn't have anything else to give besides his love; the woman asked what it was and he answered that it was passion fruit.

"It's disgusting!" shrieked the woman and threw it away, because she didn't love the man.

If she had loved him, she would have eaten it and said that it was lovely.

I bought the passion fruit on sale. It coast one mark, sixty pennies, and weighed one hundred grams. As I was buying it, I thought that people make their own suffering, even though they think that it's caused by others. I thought about Alexander, who told me yesterday that Vera had asked him to come to her, and that he's going there for Christmas.

Speaking of which, in the sky in the backyard the enormous sign of grief is visible again. If Jesus had been hanged, it would have been a gallows. Every evening the same light comes on and burns through the night. A man sins under it, if you want to call it a sin. It's more an aesthetic nuisance, but a devout Christian might consider it blasphemy. The man exposes himself under the cross. He lives on the top floor and maybe doesn't know anything about it. During the day he's an upstanding family man. He goes to work at the stock market, a bank, or a government office. He has a wife and two children. On Saturday he beats the rugs in the backyard, washes his car, goes shopping at the K-Market, and carries packages of Lenina diapers into the house. Every night, though, an evil spirit enters him. He turns on the spotlight and starts his show. Maybe his marriage is unhappy, or his Venus rotates backwards, and he can't do anything to control his passions. I don't know who the object is, or how long the relationship has been going on, because it was only this fall that I noticed it, when the leaves fell from the poplars in the yard, revealing this man in such a strange and startling light.

I seldom look out the window to the backyard. Nothing interesting happens there. It represents the reverse side of the soul. From the window onto the front yard, you can see that the wheels of society are turning. Delivery trucks drive back and forth on the road, women who have been shopping in the city exit blue busses and on the opposite hill a man stands holding a red and white stick making signs to another man. The man and the measuring stick are a sign that the landscape will be changing in a while. A new building or parking lot will come or the road will be widened.

{ 22 } Today is like a heavy train car that I have to start moving with nothing but brute force. I wonder whether it's worth it to get up at all. Less food will be consumed if I stay in bed, and I won't have the trouble of putting on clothes. Undressing is easier than dressing. The cat sits on the corner of the nightstand and watches while I read the paper. In a way it's unemployed too, because it can't get out to hunt mice, but she doesn't turn it into a moral problem the way I do. She watches me, looking as though she's asking whether I'll get up and give her some herring. In my childhood home there was a cat that didn't like Eino Railo's literary history or Ibsen's *Brand*. He tore them up and made a litter box for himself from the shreds. He could have been a literary critic.

In the newspaper it says that unemployment kills. On Granada TV on Wednesday they interviewed Professor Harvey Brenner, who has researched the matter scientifically. The unemployed agree with him. They told about the effects of unemployment at home: my son couldn't stand it and hanged himself, the wife needs tranquilizers, and a neighbor is suffering from cirrhosis of the liver. What's going on with *my* neighbor? She's gotten up on the wrong side of the bed again and is bellowing on the telephone.

"Goddammit, I got my griefs too and I ain't gone beggin' for comfort. No point in you whimpering about it."

Grandmothers didn't used to curse. They sat in rocking chairs and told fairytales to their grandchildren. Nowadays they get raging drunk. One evening I saw a bunch of them being unloaded from a Black Mariah in front of the Töölö police station. They waved their canes menacingly and slandered the policemen. Maybe they were from some old-folks home. They'd made some moonshine and started to fight and break the furniture.

The clock strikes eleven times next door. My former coworkers are going on their lunch break; I'm just planning to get up. I get dressed and go to the store to buy herring for the cat. Every day the same old men and women stand around the K-Market's slot machines. You never see young people there. Two women in the checkout line are discussing why women are so aggressive these days. One thinks it's due to living in high-rise apartment buildings. The higher up a woman lives, the angrier she becomes. I don't face that danger, since I live on the first floor. The Earth's gravity has something to do with it, but I don't hear what it is, because their turn comes to pay.

A young man is distributing leaflets in front of the K-Market and asks whether I believe in Jesus. No woman has ever asked me that. Perhaps they've agreed that men will save women and women save men, since people are more responsive to the allure of the opposite sex. The young man holds out a leaflet and says that Jesus loves me. It doesn't comfort me. There are lots of saviors running around these days. A doomsday preacher at Simonkenttä announced that false prophets are springing up all over—they speak in His name, but He isn't any of them, because His coming will be like a bolt of lightning from east to west. Two Jehovah's Witnesses come to my door a couple times a month and the cat runs between their legs into the stairwell. I say that I don't have time to listen since the evil spirit ran away and I have to catch him. They return faithfully time after time. Are they striving for a place in heaven or are they doing it altruistically, out of pure love for their neighbor? I'm beginning to suspect that either I look especially miserable, or else I've become the target of a concerted attack by the spiritual powers, since they're constantly trying to save me. But it happens to other people, too. One day in the streetcar I heard a young man forcing some leaflet on a girl standing next to him, saying, "Repent, follow Jesus throughout your life and he'll forgive your sins."

"I don't have very many sins," the girl said, and blushed.

{ 23 } The wind is blowing from the north. It hurls little shards of ice at the window, and the cat watches with her ears pricked up. Next door the wall clock strikes twice. The telephone rings in the kitchen. This is the time of night when the infatuated man calls, drunk because he's been quarreling with his girlfriend and she's driven him out of her house. Now he's sitting in his bachelor pad in a threadbare armchair, the cork open on the third bottle of wine, remembering the time when he was sixteen years old and I seduced him behind a red barn somewhere in Porkkalanniemi. In his life he's obeyed the Bible's instruction not to cast off the beloved of your youth, and it has only brought him sorrow. He calls to remind me that I deserted him, broke the engagement even though we were supposed to get married and never separate. He says, "Why did you stop loving me?"

"Because I fell in love with somebody else!"

"Have you ever really loved anybody?"

"What do you mean 'really'?"

He becomes pathetic, says that he hasn't stopped loving me.

He drags out all kinds of things he would never be cruel enough to mention when he's sober: that I destroyed his life, swindled him and gave empty promises, deceived and tormented him. He's called three nights in a row to say the same things. I don't understand how he can tell that things are going badly for me just at the right time to offer a shoulder for me to cry on. Is there an invisible connection between us? According to a Chinese folktale, a man who lives in the moon ties cords to the legs of people who are meant for each other: they can't escape, unavoidably stumbling across each other sooner or later. I've known Jussi for twenty-two years, seven of which I was engaged to him. He doesn't give me a chance to forget, even though forgetting would be best for him. Usually the less you remember a person, the nicer they become. Unpleasant characteristics fall out of your memory like rubbish. He reminds me of the awful time when I was a fiancée, went on a jealous rampage with a bread knife, hung naked around his knees and listened with my ear to his mail slot to see whether I could hear another woman's voice. He brought out all of my worst qualities. Maybe it was love. Women liked him, he had such a large head and sad eyes. He attracted women who took pity on suffering creatures, the ones who as children took such tender care of birds with injured legs or wings that they died, and as adults spent years protecting and trying to save their drunken husbands, until finally they became frustrated and turned into feminists. He also made an impression on my mother; perhaps they were companions in wretchedness in some previous life, because even when he was young he already looked born to suffer. When I became engaged to him, I watched my dreams carelessly and didn't understand them. I didn't know the I Ching yet, which I could have consulted for guidance. Mother thought I was getting a faithful man in him, and she was right: he's been faithful in the way men are, that they love one, but go to bed with many. When I hear his drunken voice on the telephone, my natural affability is put to the test. He nags at my guilty conscience, but then I get indignant and I think, "Let him go hang himself." I don't say it out loud, because he might actually do it. As a former naval officer, he can make strong knots—it wouldn't go as well for him as for Madame N., who went to the forest with the intention of hanging herself but couldn't tie a proper knot, as the doctor declared dryly. Since then, I've thought of suicide as a practical activity, and practicality isn't for me. Jussi offers me his eternal and undying love on the telephone. It makes me furious, and I slam down the receiver in his ear. He can still get to me. He isn't just anybody; he knows me and that makes me furious with him.

Ten minutes later the telephone rings again insistently. I don't answer it anymore, unplugging the cord from the wall. I look through the window at the snow-covered trees. The landscape is like a postcard. An old-fashioned dump truck with a snowplow attached to the front clatters along the street.

Wishes come true too late. When I wished he would call, he didn't; now he calls so much that I lose sleep at night. I think about how the trouble and misery of loving are known well enough, but has anyone written about the pain of being the object of love? Rilke's phrase comes to mind: "To be loved is to pass away, to love is to endure." He must have experienced how suffocating it is to be loved, because he wrote about a Prodigal Son who ran away from home because he couldn't endure his family's tenderness anymore; his sensitive soul was even tormented by the loving dogs, whose eyes reflected discernment and sympathy, expectation and concern, and he decided resolutely that he would never love, that he would never put anyone in the horrible position of being loved. Of course he forgot about his decision, and he even returned home, but we don't know whether he stayed there. Rilke speculates that it probably felt indescribably liberating to him when everyone at home misunderstood him.

{ 24 } I woke up in a gloomy mood. During the night I gave birth to a child in a stable, but I don't remember if it was a girl or boy, or even if it survived. The clock strikes eight times on the other side of the wall. Water started to run, the neighbor got into the bath, a door slammed in the hallway. I got up, put the tea water on the burner, and plugged the telephone into the wall. It rang immediately. Jussi was calling, saying he was sober now. The canaries twittered cozily in the background. He'd been forgiven and gotten back under the protection of his girlfriend's wings. He asked whether I would go sailing with him.

"What lunatic would go sailing in winter?"

"Let's go in the summer."

"No."

"Don't you like me at all?" he asked in the world's most pathetic voice, making me feel as though I was the villain.

I said I could start liking him if he would stop calling. I ended the call by wishing him a merry Christmas. I'll never forget his affection; he brooded over me like an egg and was shocked when a creature emerged from the egg that had legs and wanted to flee his love. I no longer feel the need to return to the grim state of being loved. I've gotten out twice, knock on wood that it doesn't happen a third time. His call is like a net that a fisherman throws in the same place he's caught fish before.

From the other side of the street I can hear the voices of the Christmas tree salesmen. They talk and tell anecdotes to warm themselves, bursting into laughter like people do in the South. Finns know how to laugh too, but I still haven't grown so old that I could enjoy this country in the winter. The yellow-red sun has risen to light up the wall. I calculated that during the night thirty-two blossoms have emerged on the Christmas cactus—the same number of knife wounds in the woman's body that Alexander found in his dream.

"What about it?" he asked resignedly when he woke up.

This happened the morning before last; in the evening he left to see his wife. Now my throat is sore and my head aches. I'm coming down with the flu. Whenever he goes to see Vera, I get sick. I can't get up, I stare and wonder whether they'll separate. They've been apart for so long that it's turned into a way of life. For his part there isn't any fear of being loved in return. He isn't jealous, doesn't complain about my dreams, doesn't read my diaries, doesn't condemn or criticize, doesn't tell me I'm stupid. Instead, he listens to what I say. He's friendly and tender and doesn't reveal his bad sides. Often he's sad, because he knows that I'm only an intermediate stage, like so many women have been, and that he'll abandon me on the day that Vera finally comes. He won't abandon Vera whatever she might do or say, betray and lie or behave in a way that would never be forgiven in a man. Vera treats him just as badly as I treated Jussi—tears and mangles him—but it doesn't diminish his love. Is love anything more than torment, a state of humiliation that a man endures from time to time? A woman is a man's cross, and hanging on the cross is the best-known form of loving in Western countries. It's an example; we have to strive toward it, because whoever abases himself is raised up, said he who was killed and whose birthday will be celebrated again the day after tomorrow.

{ 25 } The room smells like the forest because of the Christmas tree. It's standing sideways and is lopsided like a person who is half-paralyzed. I felt sorry for it because it seemed so ostracized; people went past and didn't see it even though it was reaching out its branches toward them. They want their Christmas trees to be beautiful, but I specialize in the ugly ones. The feeling of pity becomes burdensome in time, especially if it's directed toward people. Christmas trees aren't as mean as ugly people who have been betrayed too many times in their lives. I went outside; a bunch of young people had been at the evening service and were making a lot of noise in front of the church. It's the only place that's open on Christmas. I walked along the streets and thought that sadness is a hereditary disease. I have this sadness of Mother's in me, which doesn't have any cause. There was water squelching in the gutters the way it does in March and there was the thud of snow sliding off of roofs onto the ground. I ate some ginger snaps, which are burned at the edges and have a bitter flavor. Every year I make pastries and ginger snaps, but they never taste good. Making them is fun, but when the final product comes out, I don't enjoy it. I light some candles—it wards off evil. That's why churches keep eternal flames. During the Christmas season lots of invisible things are abroad and not all of them have good intentions.

Unrequited love tears at the heart. It has nine lives like a cat, and it doesn't end even if it's ended. Marriage kills love. That's why people get married. They escape from that feeling of torment and their minds are freed to think about other things. When I'm sober I open a box of matches the wrong way and all the matches fall onto the floor, like just now. When I'm drunk I don't make mistakes like that. I've made the greatest mistakes of my life when I was sober, but I don't want to remember them now. Can you call falling in love sobriety? A sort of twilight state takes over the brain, even in a woman. It takes me a full day to recover after I've been at Alexander's for the night. My head doesn't feel like my own, and it isn't my own; there are foreign thoughts and images in it. In the paper it said that in the future it will be possible to clean out a person's brain partially or completely and then load it with information and ideas from another person's memory. I had a dream that a wolf was tearing to pieces a sleeping man who had disguised himself as a wolf. After I woke up, I thought the wolf was Vera. I don't think of myself as bad, even though I'm the author of my dreams and in them I've killed men in cold blood. They've all been strangers, except for the man upstairs who resembles Jussi. A childhood friend of mine caught him on his fishing line, asked what to do with him, and I said to throw him off the balcony. We threw him down to the street from the fifth floor.

Someone slams a car door shut in the yard. I looked to see if it was Santa Claus, but it wasn't. There's a coconut on the floor—it's like a child's skull—and gold ribbons glisten on the Christmas tree. I don't know why, but when I think of Alexander, I'm reminded of the school history book picture of Henry VIII, who had bad luck with his wives. He had to kill them when he couldn't get away from them any other way. Alexander has the same round cheeks, but his eyes are more beautiful, except for right now, because he's squinting one eye in my imagination, and looking at the invisible cards in his hand. He looks like an old gambler. He said that he wouldn't go to Vera's anymore, but he went anyway. Every time he comes from seeing her, he says that it was the last time. There's a wooden mask on his face, and he isn't himself, or rather what I think he is, since how can I know what he really is?—I see him through own moods, and they are always changing.

Saturn, who distorts relationships, lives in the House of Love. If it marries the moon, it will become a nag; if it marries the sun, it will get an inferiority complex; if Mars, it will become jealous and frigid, withdrawing into its shell and sulking like a crayfish in a hole in the rock. It cuts off the testicles of Uranus and throws them into the sea. Venus is born from the semen and the Three Furies from the blood. It wants to bind Venus to itself legally. It castrated its father and eats its children, but one child conquers it. The child's name is Jupiter, who is my protector, and I don't need to be afraid of anything if I have faith in him. Faith? This is written in stars that aren't visible tonight, tonight when He has no crib for His bed, the little Lord Jesus who lays down His sweet head.

{ 26 } Three women in black hats visited me in a dream. Three daughters of the night named the Spinner, the Drawer of Lots, and the Inevitable. The brims of their hats shaded their faces, and they said nothing. Not even the day's paper presents a solution to the problem of existence. It comes again, showing what Man did on Christmas. He's shot another man dead in Riihimäki, turned up frozen to death in the snow in Jämsä, died in a house fire in Nakkila, walked in front of a car in Sonkajärvi, broke into a house in Raisio, stabbed someone in Lahti, and died in a head-on collision in Kangasniemi. Christmas was a difficult time for him, and he didn't make it out alive. They don't tell about Woman in the paper. She set the table, cooked the food, made coffee, washed the dished, visited with relatives, hid her husband's bottles, and wept because of him. It snowed overnight. Bobcat, a small white snowplow with the picture of a cat on its side, is rolling around the yard. Today the day is one minute longer than yesterday; the journey toward summer is beginning. It's the time of the year when I can't sleep and can't stay awake. I'm like Oblomov: I yawn, stretch, turn over on my side, and doze off. Every morning I'm worried about the state of my soul, since I don't accomplish anything. The mother of all sins is laziness; will I have to live in this purgatory for very long? Jesus said, "Behold the fowls of the air: for they sow not, neither do they reap, nor gather into barns. The flowers of the field do not labor, neither do they spin." Jesus recommended following their example. I've tried to follow his advice. Every day they talk on the radio about Jesus's works, even though two thousand years have passed since his death. You hear less about Buddha. He wasn't as powerful a magician as Jesus, who conjured water into wine and fed five thousand people with five loaves and two fishes. Would the world economy collapse if people like him were born more often? He had a propensity for quick-temperedness. His astrological chart had Mars and Uranus in a square. When he was hungry, he was irritable like any man. When there were only leaves on a fig tree and no fruit, because it wasn't their season, he became angry and said, "May you never bear any fruit," and the tree withered on the spot. The disciples wondered at this; he was embarrassed by his quick temper and explained as best he could, that if they had faith, and not doubt, then they would receive everything they wanted—if they told a mountain rise up and cast thyself into the sea, then the mountain would do it. His Mars was in the ninth house, which meant that he was politically and religiously ambitious; he had the ability to lead an ideological movement and a resolute manner of spreading his faith to large groups of people. His Pluto was in opposition with Saturn. It meant persecution and a violent death. The

Magi from the East didn't know Pluto, Neptune and Uranus, but they saw from the position of the stars that the king of the Jews was born in Bethlehem on the third day of October in the year 7 B.C. at 3:41 in the afternoon, and they went to worship him. They were wise men, but they weren't wise enough to keep their mouths shut. Jesus interests me, because we have in common that his moon and Uranus, as well as his Jupiter and Saturn, unite in the sign of Pisces. They unite for me too, but in Taurus and the House of Love. I'm not cut out to be an ascetic like him. I don't understand the spiritual side of love and I'm no good at abstaining from sensual pleasures. I like everything that can be touched with the hand, heard with the ear, seen with the eye, and tasted with the tongue. I like having a man inside me, the touch of silk and velvet on my skin, salmon and caviar in my mouth. I couldn't tell the devil no if he came to the summit the mountain to tempt me and promised me dominion over the entire world if I would surrender to him. Afterward I would be very repentant.

The cat is asleep under the Christmas tree and a suitcase is squeaking in the closet. During the night it fell down and startled me awake. I'm reading Yeats and thinking that a person has to experience all sorts of mental agony before she becomes an adult. He admitted feeling very ashamed of his sexuality.

I'm beginning to feel drowsy. When I'm half-asleep an image comes into my mind of the fat whore who sits on the stone step in front of the staircase of the next building over. She smokes Salems. She has white angel curls, which sparkle like a halo around her head when the sun shines on her hair. She has red toenails and strap-sandals. She yawns and I see her tongue and the roof of her mouth, which are pink, like other people's, but she isn't like other people, she's much more interesting because people say she's a whore who works at the harbor. I'm twelve years old; I've read the part in the Bible where it tells about Aholah and Aholibah. Secret dealings between men and women have started to interest me. I only have indirect knowledge of them. I know how gulls and cats mate, but I don't have a clear picture of how it happens between people. To me the whore is very beautiful and enviable; she knows the sorts of things that I don't, and she's an adult, or at least I consider her an adult. She's maybe seventeen or eighteen years old. Her image disappears and when I wake up my head is clear, there's no pain and no depression, it feels exceptional. The sky has descended to the pine tree's branches. Snow whirls at a slant past the window and the snowplows rumble on the street. The ground is absolutely white, not a stain from any activity. A small dog wallows happily in the snow, and its master stands in the shelter of the pine's trunk with his collar turned up. I think you can't say very much bad about men and women. Together they make each other's lives miserable, but they aren't happy when they're apart, either. I still haven't experienced what it's like when there's mutual love between a man and a woman. Does it exist? Spirit loves spirit and body loves body. Alexander takes care of my body's needs and leaves my heart alone. The body gets what it desires, but the spirit thirsts for more. It's grasping and insatiable and nothing will satisfy its yearning except intercourse with God. I guess I'm some kind of mystic. I don't have it in me to become a cynic. You become a real cynic by extinguishing all lust and submitting to the guidance of fate, taught Epictetus.

{ 27 } I looked at the future by pouring melted tin in cold water on New Year's Eve. I saw a small woman with a long shadow. It was Vera. She went crazy, but not the way that I'm crazy—I don't reveal it to anyone and don't disturb the environment because I don't want to end up in the madhouse, having worked there and seen what it's like. She couldn't endure unemployment and money worries anymore. Her nerves snapped, she flew off the handle and started throwing dishes at the walls. Her doctor-mother realized that she was crazy, which the mother had suspected ever since Vera had, to the shame of her relatives, suddenly gotten married to a foreigner. Her mother had her committed to a mental hospital. At first I didn't believe it, but Alexander's son confirmed that she was quite nuts. He'd seen with his own eyes that there were bars on the windows and the doors were locked, but in his opinion Vera wasn't crazy, just very angry. She'd thrown the presents in their faces when they went to the hospital. She didn't have to languish there very long: after a week she was already better or at least got to go home. Was she pacified by the straitjacket or hot and cold baths? And what was the diagnosis when she was admitted? Did the papers say hypochondria? I was awake all night thinking about her. What sort of person is she? I wondered, and looked at her stars. They were the same as Mother's. She had weak health and a poor relationship with her own mother. She feared her own sensuality, suppressed it and deceived men, because they didn't live up to her dreams. She dreamed of a man who would be as tender as a dove and cunning as a serpent, but she didn't meet any men like that. She had no happiness in love. Her good stars were in the House of the Homeland. She wavered in the area between insanity and hysteria, because she couldn't choose the lesser of the two evils, whether to remain in misery in her homeland, watched over by her pious and detestable mother, or go to her husband, whom she no longer loved, and had probably never loved. Alexander blames himself, as all decent people do when their closest relatives have been stricken with misfortune. Maybe it's caused by the stars. Her stars were in bad positions in the sky. Uranus was in a square with her Saturn, her Mars and her moon. During the times of such bad intersections many people probably end up behind bars, but it gets blamed on bad conditions at home or on their genes.

"A man's good or bad luck comes through a woman," an Irish god, whose name I don't remember, said to a young man when he asked what he should do. The god urged him to get married. *Deus ex machina*, I think about Vera's going mad. I won't start competing with a lunatic for a man, because the lunatic always wins, and I only play to win.

My day begins when I throw out the Christmas tree. I haven't had time to form an empathetic relationship with it. Sometimes it's been hard to part with a Christmas tree, when it's started to throw out green top shoots. I have a strange habit of getting attached to trees, animals, children, and men. I wouldn't want to give them up. I mourned for the angelfish, too, when it died after suffering persecution in the last moments of its life. It was a calm fish, a philosopher by nature. It moved slowly around the aquarium, dignified, like my grandmother. It didn't recognize its children, instead it ate them. In a way I'm to blame for its death, because I put the good-for-nothing tiger barb with the character disorder in the aquarium.

A pneumatic drill is beating in the street. It started at 8:00. The department of transportation sent it to my window as a wake-up call. The elections are coming. I hear a faint rustling and a white card floats from the mail slot onto the rug: a flyer about voter's rights. I'm a citizen of this country; I can vote for the president. The wooden billboards have appeared along the streets with the pictures of the candidates. Why isn't there any wide, motherly woman among the candidates, or an ethereal muse who glides around in diaphanous veils like Isadora Duncan?

A light snow is falling. Two men are walking on the roof of the neighboring building, admiring the landscape, and some invisible being unscrews a lightbulb from its socket. I hear a grating sound. That's its way of expressing itself, just like a cat has the habit of meowing and I have the habit of writing. Luckily the invisible person doesn't speak; otherwise I'd think I was going insane. When I heard the sound for the first time, I thought the neighbor on the other side of the wall was putting in a new lightbulb to replace one that had burned out, but when the grating just continued, I came to the conclusion that her lightbulbs couldn't burn out every day. Perhaps the lightbulb switcher was Marek Sokolowski, a Polish citizen I live with in some sort of common-law marriage arrangement. The super came to say that I had to register him. Apparently there was a call from the police department saying that he wasn't on the building's records, even though he'd been at my address for three months already. I said that I'd never even seen him. Suspicion flashed in the super's eyes: women always say that.

One night some mute man stood next to my bed, his arms folded across his chest like an Egyptian mummy. It was so dark that I couldn't really see what kind of man he was, and when I woke up he was gone. One morning I found a short piece of string with a slip of paper dangling at the end in my bed; on the paper it read, "In a way, everyone loves his own. A proverb from Kangasa." It was from a Princess tea bag. Was it Marek's profession of love? Was it he who put the golden ring in the sewing box? Was it he who hid my things?—especially my fountain pen, the one I write my notes with in the morning? Was it he who broke my typewriter? It squeaked like someone had stuck it with a pin, a red light flashed on the left side, and it stopped working. I pressed the button that makes it fix itself automatically, but nothing happened. Some junk had gotten into the display card, which had caused a short circuit. The man at the repair shop said that he hadn't encountered a problem like this before, and he didn't understand how it was possible for dirt to get in there. Removing the dirt cost three hundred, a new fuse, eighteen marks. I sold the television to get the money, so now I can't see the Iran-Iraq war or the problems in Palestine, and momentarily the world seems to be a better place to live in. I guess Marek doesn't like that I write. Men generally don't like it if their woman concentrates too much on anything other than them. They feel neglected and become jealous. I don't know where or when our relationship started, and I don't recall having met anyone from Poland. Could there be such a thing as one-sided introductions, just like one-sided love? He's the first man with whom I've had a guaranteed spiritual relationship. No matter how much a relationship like that between a man and woman is valued by the world, I don't understand what pleasure there is in it.

I'm also gradually starting to grow invisible. Acquaintances no longer greet me when they walk by on the street. Today the clerk at the fish counter looked straight through me, even though I was the only customer. He picked his nose and went to the back room to cut up some dog bones or to flirt with his female colleague. At the bread counter I became invisible in the middle of making a purchase. I bought a roll, and the saleswoman put it into a bag, then I asked for one of the doughnuts that were on sale. Without saying a word, the saleswoman left to stack packages of bread on the shelf. I walked after her and asked, "What about my doughnut?"

She acted startled, as though I'd materialized out of thin air.

{ 28 } I had a dream about getting a job as a newspaper carrier. I thought that I'd call in sick, but my sense of responsibility won out. The papers were heavy and the area unfamiliar, just warehouses and industrial buildings. Dreams seldom come true immediately, but this one did. There was a call from the employment office and the person asked in a stern tone whether I wanted to work at all. I said that I did, if they had a decent offer, none of the newspaper circulation or Cygnaeus museum guard/cleaner drudgery they offered me last time. They had a one-year position in a vocational training center, in other words, an unemployment training center, but you can't use that term because there aren't any unemployed. Everyone is a worker-to-be. The Minister of Education was coming to dedicate a new building and they needed a public relations officer. Someone had noticed that they didn't have one, and now there was only week left before the Minister's visit. My new career didn't begin very well. The Minister came and delivered a speech, and the building was dedicated, but not one newspaper was there. Some young guy came from the radio and I got him lost in a building I didn't know.

I don't have any official function at the training center. I sit in the doorway and pass the time. Yesterday a Chinese man, Dixin Tsang, and his wife, Ming Tsang, paid a visit. I told them about the center's objectives and program of instruction, comporting myself with distinction and giving a positive picture of my place of employment. Mr. Tsang was a reporter for a Beijing newspaper. He said that it's a small paper: there are only six million readers. Today I wrote a three-page piece about advanced and in-service training for welding teachers, a subject I know nothing about and don't have the slightest interest in. In my way I'm also a newspaper carrier, because I edit the internal newsletter and distribute it once a week to the teachers' mailboxes. I don't know whether they read it. No one says anything, even though I put nasty aphorisms at the end of it. This week I borrowed from Stanislaw Jerzy Lecia: "When everything has to be in its place, there's probably something awry." In selecting the aphorism, I was thinking of the director, who can't stand disorder. He says that visitors get the wrong image of an office when there's paper all over the place in the copy room. The teachers were asking me what kind of man the new director is. Is he a teetotaler, since he said at the department-head meeting that the drunks had to be removed from the commons area? The department heads asked who would do it, not the teachers of course, since it isn't in their job description, and they don't want a knife in the ribs or a fist in the face. The director said that according to the regulations, a teacher carries out the tasks that are assigned to him, and if he orders that the drunks are to be removed, the teachers have to obey that order. I can't say what kind of man he is. The center's manager says that he feels like he works in a kennel club because of the way the boss gives commands: Fetch! Take! Call! The boss from the countryside and is really still a little timid and indecisive. He spends most of his time standing in front of the window with his hands behind his back, looking outside. Maybe he's thinking about his future in vocational training administration or the Ministry of Education. I have a premonition that our relationship will not be a happy one. I make him nervous because the straight-as-an-arrow order on his desk always gets mixed up when I enter the room, even if I don't touch anything. I don't respect him enough.

{ 29 } A cloud that looks like a dog is running across the sky. I don't have a permanent place in the office; I'm still crouching in the doorway and can't see anything other than that narrow strip of sky. There's nothing else to see, just the warehouse and the shop building. I share a room with a small girl who's like an angel that accidentally fell to earth. She has blonde, cherubic curls and shy blue eyes. When she smiles, a pained expression trembles at the corners of her mouth. Her name is Taru. She's a former unemployment training course student who got a place in the office as a typist. She doesn't dare talk to me because I'm old and experienced. I have half a lifetime of horrors behind me; for her they're still ahead. She thinks that I'm doing important work when I'm drawing circles on paper. In the morning a delegation of worried university students came. They'd heard that a shantytown was being evacuated and the occupants were being transferred to their buildings. They said that they already had Iraqis living with them who were so noisy that no one could study for their exams.

It feels like a tire is being inflated around my head. I probably have delusions of grandeur, because it feels like this building is too cramped for me, that the corridors are so narrow that my elbows knock against the walls. Is this going to initiate my rebirth? My spirit doesn't want to move, the air in the room is running out. I open the door into the corridor, where I hear someone shouting into the telephone, "Are you trying to kill me out in the cold?" He speaks Finnish with a foreign accent. Taru says that the caller is an Estonian refugee who had a nervous breakdown because he's been unemployed for five years. Unemployment doesn't suit Finnic peoples; they have a saying that "Everyone is the smith of his own happiness." In contrast, the Vietnamese boat refugees seem to adjust well to the training center. They're diligent—they don't fight and they don't drink liquor. Whenever I see them in the cafeteria or the hallway, they smile happily. I think they even smile in their sleep. Are they ironists who don't take the miseries of this world seriously? Perhaps they've noticed that it's more intelligent to let fate or chance decide on their behalf. Kierkegaard wrote that for an ironist, everything is possible. He is sometimes a god, sometimes a grain of sand. Nothing is permanent for him. His feelings are as random as the incarnations of Brahma: on the way to a monastery he stops at the temple of Venus or the other way around. You shouldn't criticize him: it's difficult for him to become something, and it isn't easy to choose from an infinite number of possibilities. Kierkegaard probably had trouble deciding on a profession. When I was young I didn't understand him—I was a too serious. When I read *The Seducer's Diary*, I dismissed him indignantly, because he said that a woman lives only through a man. As a sixteen-year-old I took everything literally. I'm not a fully mature ironist even now. You have to practice, toss three coins in the air and ask the I Ching, "Shall I choose this or that?"

The director brings in a stack of papers and says, "Make an agenda." He's such a lazy man that he can't even bother to dictate proposals. He depends on my being some sort of mind reader who knows what he wants. I know that it will be proposed that a helicopter pilot's course be organized for pesticide sprayers and an airplane pilot's course for those who intend to fly commercial planes. Both courses cost millions, but what significance does money have when the unemployed need to acquire proper professions? In addition, it will be proposed that the director and the governing board be sent to London to become acquainted with their vocational training operations. The financial director won't approve it. Then it will be proposed that the financial director be sent to London too. The board won't approve that the recording secretary be taken along on the trip. I'm the recording secretary. At meetings I pour coffee into the cups, keep my mouth closed, write what I'm ordered to write, listen closely and learn that the decision-makers make decisions that are advantageous to themselves, but you can't tell the press about that. The less information people have, the better it is for the decision-makers. They can continue to make advantageous decisions without outsiders interfering in the progress of things. I'm also learning that new proposals go through right away if the right person introduces them. The right person has the right position and title.

After the board meeting I get a headache. Axes flash in my eyes; I have such murderous thoughts because I'm not a decision-maker and I can't send myself to London, where I very much want to go.

{ 30 } In the mornings and evenings I have to ride to work past Alexander's building. It squeezes my heart, and my eyes hurt when I try to see through the walls to see if Vera has come already. Today I thought about a Buñuel film where some people are imprisoned in a building. Whenever they try to leave, something incomprehensible prevents them. The name of the film is *The Exterminating Angel*. When I didn't know Alexander yet, the building didn't mean anything. I didn't look at it, but now my neck turns even though I've firmly resolved that I won't even look towards the building; I'll act as though it doesn't exist. The bus goes past so rapidly that I don't have time to see very much. Sometimes there's a light in his window, sometimes not. I don't see any people in the yard or the dog in the pen—did it die? A snow shovel leans against the wall of the shed, frozen footprints go from the well to the sauna and next to the stairs the branches of the rose bush jut out from the snow. I fell into that bush when I went to his apartment for the first time. I was bending down to smell the scent of the rose when a branch grabbed my sleeve and pulled me off my feet. I got thorns in my skin, a scrape on my ear, a bruise on my thigh, the skin came off my knee, and there were long scratches on my nose when I looked at myself in the mirror in the morning. Was the fall a portent? The I Ching forecast that a thunderstorm would rise up, lightning bolts would strike here and there and it would be impossible to avoid them, for it is the will of heaven. That sort of thing happens in the summer, when a heat wave has gone on for a long time. Desire comes so suddenly that you don't even have time to feel lust. You rush into love like an express train into a tunnel—the warning light is broken. Many years pass before the light begins to gleam again from the other end of the tunnel.

I went to the store, and a blue tit was singing, the first sign of spring, but it didn't raise my spirits. One of the brothers Karamazov said that hell was suffering because you were unable to love anymore. I fell from heaven to hell; people live here too, but I'm suffocating with longing, and it isn't any vague longing. My hands want to touch and caress a man, my mouth wants to kiss, my legs want to twine around his legs. The moon is growing full again and my desire follows the phases of the moon, like the tides. A person gets used to pleasures so easily that getting unused to them is difficult. Intercourse is the body's opium; a moment of intoxication and the consciousness expands to infinity. God probably had the devil in mind when he created man and woman and made them feel their attraction to one another. God invented the devil, too. He's God's right hand and Jesus is his left.

The devil lays snares for me to fall into. At the intersection of Huopalahti Road and Tarvo Road he threw a used condom that led my thoughts to earthly pleasures. My resolution about an ascetic life began to waver and my dreams became like those ascetics and saints usually have, so they wouldn't forget that they're only human beings. At first I struggled heroically against it. I kicked Alexander when he came to my bed and tried to take me by force. But you can't avoid temptations. It's better to yield to them immediately than to postpone them until later. The following night I'm at his place, in a room like a storehouse. The floor is full of teetering piles of books, cardboard boxes, and plastic bags, which contain his archives. On top of the cardboard cartons are piles of dirty clothes. He doesn't do laundry, just buys new clothes when the old ones get dirty. On a hook hangs a bathrobe that belonged to his wife, who died six years ago. Her slippers are under the bed and on the table dictionaries, memoranda, papers and pens are scattered around, as though his wife was coming back tomorrow to continue her interrupted work. Alexander doesn't give anything away. He wouldn't have given me up either, if I hadn't wanted him to myself. I raise my arms and wrap them around his neck, but he doesn't return the embrace. He isn't scornful or angry; maybe he's confused. I rock him in my arms; caress his skin, touch with my lips and tongue the silky surface of his penis. I turn over and climb on top of him, he sucks at my breasts, and I squeeze his scrotum in the palm of my hand. Someone says in a tender voice, "This place is haunted," and I wake up in my own bed. I feel like I visited him and that the voice is that of his son. I had probably left my body; the son saw me and thought I was a ghost.

All day there was a tune in my head, "Oh if I, a traveling man, go to the end of the world, I'll get to see you, my heart longs for you, my soul calls to you." I miss his touches and the shared mornings when I lie hand in hand with him, telling him about my dreams; he tells me his, and quiet music plays on the radio.

{ 31 } It snows every day. Sometimes it snows from the south, sometimes from the north. The signs of spring are increasing. A stupefied moth staggers out from between the pages of the book that I open and icicles lengthen on the edge of Alexander's eaves. It's March. Sometimes it fells like I can't stand it anymore, I'll go crazy with longing, but it passes when I concentrate on thinking that he's a mean person and a hypocrite. Last time he said that a kiss is only five centimeters of skin and pitied me because I imagined that it was more. Nearly three months have passed since then.

One day the longing doesn't subside, but instead torments me persistently, like an obsession. I'm coming from work and I get off the bus near Sinai, where long ago there was a dance floor. Bus No. 36, which I usually transfer to, is standing at the stop. I would have made it if I'd run, but I received a revelation that I had to go to Alexander's place. He lives about two hundred meters from the bus stop. His son comes to open the door. He isn't surprised when he sees me, instead acting as though I'd visited them only yesterday. He says that his father is sick and is sleeping.

"I'll drop by some other time," I say.

"He can wake up, he isn't that sick," the son says and invites me in. He goes to wake up his father.

He's wearing a blue robe and his eyes are red like a rabbit's. I ask what happened to him. He says that he went to visit Vera last week and got an eye infection there. It used to be that you got a sty in your eye if you peeked through a keyhole. Has he seen something that his eyes couldn't handle?

"Has Vera started to learn Finnish?" I ask.

"No. She's decided to become a poet. She asked for a type-writer, and I brought her one."

"Are you still waiting for Vera?"

He admits that he is, and a vague expression comes over his face that I can't interpret. It looks like his face is breaking into pieces. Maybe it's because of the tears of disappointment that spring to my eyes. I go to the stove and put the water on the burner. I'm bitter and envious.

I sit at the kitchen table with my coat on and my hat on my head, looking as though I didn't intend to stay. He offers some hot black-currant juice and says he's been sick since New Year's with a stubborn case of the flu and can't work, that the winter's been a heavy and difficult time and from year to year it seems to be getting worse. I don't understand men and their feelings. How can desire and affection be two such different things in them that they can love you and go to bed with someone else? A man can give you a rose, but a man's feelings often last even less time than it takes for the rose to start withering. We drink three cups of black-currant juice; I start to sweat and take off my coat. The deaf dog has woken up and comes to greet me—it remembers who I am. I rub him on the neck and head.

"Now he's happy," Alexander says.

I feel like there's nothing to say. It's a sign that at that exact moment there must be something to say. Or perhaps it's because I'm not used to talking with him at the table. In bed it would turn out better, but I can't suggest that; he would take it the wrong way anyhow. There are dirty dishes on the table, just as there always were before. The radio is new. He says that you can listen to the police band with it, and he snaps it on, but the police are silent. Next to the mirror is Botticelli's naked *Venus*, who stands shyly on a clamshell. It's an advertisement for some shipping company. I remember having a dream in which I was Venus and had testicles. A cobweb hangs in the corner. It looks as though it's been worn out with use. How many have lost their lives in it? I say that spiders are better than their reputation: not all females kill the males after mating, and the males of some spider species are relatively faithful. They can spend up to a month near the female's web. That's what it said in a book I borrowed from the library. Alexander warms up a pizza and I eat. He isn't hungry, but he waits on me out of habit. On the radio, some man is talking about a sinful woman. She is sinful because she'd had five men and not one had been her own. Jesus gave her the water of life, which made her thirst go away forever, and she never felt the urge to sin any more, says the man, as though it was a sure thing. Alexander asks how many men I've had.

Men usually ask that at the beginning, but he asks at the end. I say that there have been quite enough.

"Many have been the right one, but I haven't been right for many of them," I add, somewhat bitterly, meaning him.

The man on the radio claims that God loves even if he isn't loved in return, but humans are selfish. I get up to leave, but it's as though I've become rooted to the chair. At nine I try again, but I'm unsuccessful. I drink at least a liter of black-currant juice. At ten I have to go to the toilet. As I'm coming back I don't go to sit at the table anymore, instead staying in the doorway. He says that I was his angel for as long as it lasted.

When I leave him on the stairs, I recall that the Russians say, "God sent you my way," when they fall in love, but when the story is over they say, "The devil threw you in front of me." I can't help saying it to him. He stands on the stairs with the dog beside him. When I look back, his head is tilted in the same way as the dog's. On the way home, I think that I'm like the wholesome girl-next-door or co-worker in American movies, who's fallen in love with the hero. The hero likes her too, a little, but then the *femme fatale* appears on the scene. She comes from the sun or the moon and the hero is dazzled when he sees her for the first time, even though he sees nothing but a black shadow. Then she asks him in a husky voice to light her cigarette and the hero feels his heart leap, and from then on he's a gonner. I've thought that things like that only happen in movies, but it seems that it happens in reality, too. I just never would have believed that I'd have to play the role of the girl-next-door. I'm not at all wholesome; my hair is always in a tangle.

{ 32 } The rain patters against the windowpanes as I wake up. I sleep surprisingly well for someone who's been cast off. I've stopped having dreams. I've lost hope. It's easier to live without it; the longing seems less oppressive. Life is fair. First you abandon someone and then someone abandons you. I hear a melanchoic song through the wall. A woman is singing; the tune is familiar, but I can't make out the words. It's time to get up again for her daily humiliation. Human life is one long failure and the only real things are the humiliating ones.

This morning a woman got onto the bus who isn't a regular passenger. I already know the others: a worn-out-looking former beauty who's a clerk at the T-Grocery store, and her co-worker, a flat-hatted type dating from the 1950s, who has greasy Elvis-style hair, and a man with a black suit, who's round all over: his cheeks, lips, eyeglasses, bowler hat and the tips of his shoes. I often wonder what he could possibly do for a living; is he a chief accountant, a special investigator or an auditor in a bookkeeping office, whose mother died half a year ago? The new passenger has four children under school age, and the fifth is in her belly. The three boys' names are Jeremiah, Joshua, and Matthew. The girl is so obedient and quiet that her mother doesn't need to order her around, and I don't find out her name. The mother has a clean, reddish face, as though she'd just come from the sauna, and blonde hair cut close to her head. There is peace in her soul and in her blue eyes, and she doesn't appear stressed, even though the boys are wild. I look at her as though at a miracle.

A police van is standing in front of the door of the training center. Two uniformed policemen climb out of the car. I follow them to the office. They ask about the student affairs manager, Salo, and order that he be summoned.

"Don't tell him that the police are asking for him," says the older man.

A boy comes back a moment later accompanied by a teacher. He has on a cook's white uniform and tall hat.

"A change of clothes and off to prison," the younger policeman says.

Silently the boy goes to change his clothes, his shoulders hunched. The police don't touch him; they walk beside him, one on the left side, one on the right. I'm sorry about the boy's fate. What evil did he manage to do, such a small, thin boy? These days everything makes me worry. The torn willow branches, the grayed pile of firewood and the half-burned building along the old Hämeenlinna Road. The rabbit that gets frightened and leaps into the air when it sees me in the forest. The financial manager who strains himself to look larger and more important than he is. The director who has to argue with me over the interpretation of regulations. The office women who also work their guts out at home like insensible slaves, don't have time to read books and aren't interested in anything other than gossip. A short poem that I read a couple of weeks ago. It was by Yeats, only seven lines long and simple, like a folk song. The poet was grieving about his lost love. He met a beautiful woman and wished that the old desperation would give way for a new love, but it didn't happen that way. The woman looked at his heart and went away weeping because she had seen the image of another woman there. Yeats wrote in his memoirs that he was still grieving, even years later, over not being able to love that woman, who had been close to him, because Maud Gonne, for whom he had waited thirty years, had been in his heart. He said that all our lives we long for our own destruction, because we're waiting for something to happen, for next spring and summer to come, for a woman to come into our life, and we complain that destruction comes too slowly.

A familiar-looking girl comes toward me on the stairs. I haven't seen her before; maybe she's a new student. She stops and I also stop. For a moment we look at each other, and then I ask her if I've met her somewhere. She doesn't recall having met me.

"Where are you from?"

"From Pori," she says.

I've never been there, but I still feel like I've seen the girl somewhere. An image comes to mind of a dark room with many people. The girl is among them. She's unhappy. It has to do with some love affair that ended unhappily. I can't remember anything more. In my heart I have this odd sensation, a kind of twitching, as though some stitches were being pulled out. The wound has probably healed up, since the sensation of pressure, which lasted for months, is gone, and my heart feels lighter and more open. It may be that it's only a temporary phenomenon. I'll fall in love again soon with someone unsuitable, and the feeling of pressure will begin again. I'm stupid in that way: I don't become wiser through experience.

I go to my room, look at the white walls and think about the day's work. The newsletter will take an hour. Then I'll continue planning the personnel training program. When I get that ready, I don't have anything more to do in this building, if I don't invent some work for myself. Maybe I'll start planning a new employment program for the nation.

In the evening I go to the shore at Mätäoja to listen to the nightingales. I calculate that it knows twenty different languages. It doesn't stake its whole heart on one, like the stupid chaffinch that always warbles the same thing. During the night I move to a new apartment. From the window I can see a lake, on the shore of which sits a man, fishing. He's been sitting there a long time, but he hasn't caught a single fish. I go to the shore, cast a hook into the water and immediately catch a large bass, even though there's no worm on the hook.

SELECTED DALKEY ARCHIVE PAPERBACKS

FOR A FULL LIST OF PUBLICATIONS, VISIT:
www.dalkeyarchive.com

SELECTED DALKEY ARCHIVE PAPERBACKS

CAROLE MASO, *AVA.*
LADISLAV MATEJKA AND KRYSTYNA POMORSKA, EDS.,
　Readings in Russian Poetics: Formalist and
　Structuralist Views.
HARRY MATHEWS,
　The Case of the Persevering Maltese: Collected Essays.
　Cigarettes.
　The Conversions.
　The Human Country: New and Collected Stories.
　The Journalist.
　My Life in CIA.
　Singular Pleasures.
　The Sinking of the Odradek Stadium.
　Tlooth.
　20 Lines a Day.
ROBERT L. MCLAUGHLIN, ED.,
　Innovations: An Anthology of Modern &
　Contemporary Fiction.
STEVEN MILLHAUSER, *The Barnum Museum.*
　In the Penny Arcade.
RALPH J. MILLS, JR., *Essays on Poetry.*
OLIVE MOORE, *Spleen.*
NICHOLAS MOSLEY, *Accident.*
　Assassins.
　Catastrophe Practice.
　Children of Darkness and Light.
　The Hesperides Tree.
　Hopeful Monsters.
　Imago Bird.
　Impossible Object.
　Inventing God.
　Judith.
　Look at the Dark.
　Natalie Natalia.
　Serpent.
　The Uses of Slime Mould: Essays of Four Decades.
WARREN F. MOTTE, JR.,
　Fables of the Novel: French Fiction since 1990.
　Oulipo: A Primer of Potential Literature.
YVES NAVARRE, *Our Share of Time.*
　Sweet Tooth.
DOROTHY NELSON, *In Night's City.*
　Tar and Feathers.
WILFRIDO D. NOLLEDO, *But for the Lovers.*
FLANN O'BRIEN, *At Swim-Two-Birds.*
　At War.
　The Best of Myles.
　The Dalkey Archive.
　Further Cuttings.
　The Hard Life.
　The Poor Mouth.
　The Third Policeman.
CLAUDE OLLIER, *The Mise-en-Scène.*
PATRIK OUŘEDNÍK, *Europeana.*
FERNANDO DEL PASO, *Palinuro of Mexico.*
ROBERT PINGET, *The Inquisitory.*
　Mahu or The Material.
　Trio.
RAYMOND QUENEAU, *The Last Days.*
　Odile.
　Pierrot Mon Ami.
　Saint Glinglin.
ANN QUIN, *Berg.*
　Passages.
　Three.
　Tripticks.
ISHMAEL REED, *The Free-Lance Pallbearers.*
　The Last Days of Louisiana Red.
　Reckless Eyeballing.
　The Terrible Threes.
　The Terrible Twos.
　Yellow Back Radio Broke-Down.
JULIÁN RÍOS, *Larva: A Midsummer Night's Babel.*
　Poundemonium.
AUGUSTO ROA BASTOS, *I the Supreme.*
JACQUES ROUBAUD, *The Great Fire of London.*

Hortense in Exile.
Hortense Is Abducted.
The Plurality of Worlds of Lewis.
The Princess Hoppy.
The Form of a City Changes Faster, Alas,
　Than the Human Heart.
Some Thing Black.
LEON S. ROUDIEZ, *French Fiction Revisited.*
VEDRANA RUDAN, *Night.*
LYDIE SALVAYRE, *The Company of Ghosts.*
　The Lecture.
LUIS RAFAEL SÁNCHEZ, *Macho Camacho's Beat.*
SEVERO SARDUY, *Cobra & Maitreya.*
NATHALIE SARRAUTE, *Do You Hear Them?*
　Martereau.
　The Planetarium.
ARNO SCHMIDT, *Collected Stories.*
　Nobodaddy's Children.
CHRISTINE SCHUTT, *Nightwork.*
GAIL SCOTT, *My Paris.*
JUNE AKERS SEESE,
　Is This What Other Women Feel Too?
　What Waiting Really Means.
AURELIE SHEEHAN, *Jack Kerouac Is Pregnant.*
VIKTOR SHKLOVSKY, *Knight's Move.*
　A Sentimental Journey: Memoirs 1917-1922.
　Theory of Prose.
　Third Factory.
　Zoo, or Letters Not about Love.
JOSEF ŠKVORECKÝ,
　The Engineer of Human Souls.
CLAUDE SIMON, *The Invitation.*
GILBERT SORRENTINO, *Aberration of Starlight.*
　Blue Pastoral.
　Crystal Vision.
　Imaginative Qualities of Actual Things.
　Mulligan Stew.
　Pack of Lies.
　The Sky Changes.
　Something Said.
　Splendide-Hôtel.
　Steelwork.
　Under the Shadow.
W. M. SPACKMAN, *The Complete Fiction.*
GERTRUDE STEIN, *Lucy Church Amiably.*
　The Making of Americans.
　A Novel of Thank You.
PIOTR SZEWC, *Annihilation.*
STEFAN THEMERSON, *Hobson's Island.*
　Tom Harris.
JEAN-PHILIPPE TOUSSAINT, *Television.*
ESTHER TUSQUETS, *Stranded.*
DUBRAVKA UGRESIC, *Lend Me Your Character.*
　Thank You for Not Reading.
MATI UNT, *Things in the Night.*
ELOY URROZ, *The Obstacles.*
LUISA VALENZUELA, *He Who Searches.*
BORIS VIAN, *Heartsnatcher.*
PAUL WEST, *Words for a Deaf Daughter & Gala.*
CURTIS WHITE, *America's Magic Mountain.*
　The Idea of Home.
　Memories of My Father Watching TV.
　Monstrous Possibility: An Invitation to
　Literary Politics.
　Requiem.
DIANE WILLIAMS, *Excitability: Selected Stories.*
　Romancer Erector.
DOUGLAS WOOLF, *Wall to Wall.*
　Ya! & John-Juan.
PHILIP WYLIE, *Generation of Vipers.*
MARGUERITE YOUNG, *Angel in the Forest.*
　Miss MacIntosh, My Darling.
REYOUNG, *Unbabbling.*
ZORAN ŽIVKOVIĆ, *Hidden Camera.*
LOUIS ZUKOFSKY, *Collected Fiction.*
SCOTT ZWIREN, *God Head.*

FOR A FULL LIST OF PUBLICATIONS, VISIT:
w w w . d a l k e y a r c h i v e . c o m